REAL WORLD

REAL WORLD NATSUO KIRINO

TRANSLATED BY PHILIP GABRIEL

ALFRED A. KNOPF NEW YORK 2008

CONTENTS

In Japan the school year begins in April and ends in March of the following year. It consists of three terms, separated by short vacations in the spring and winter, as well as a monthlong summer break. Students attend elementary school for six years, middle school for three years, and high school for three years.

REAL WORLD

I'm penciling in my eyebrows when the smog alert siren starts blaring. It's happened every day since summer vacation started, so it's no surprise. "May I have your attention," this woman's voice drawls over a loudspeaker. "An air pollution advisory has just been issued," and the siren continues to drone on, like some kindly old dinosaur groaning away.

Most of these advisories happen in the morning, usually just as I'm about to leave for cram school. Nobody does anything because of them. Everyone kind of goes, Oh, *that* again. What I'd like to know is where they hide those speakers. To me, that's creepier and weirder than anything about smog.

I live in a crowded residential area on the outskirts of Suginami-ku in Tokyo. It used to be a nice, laid-back neighborhood, but all the old, larger houses got torn down, replaced by smaller single-family homes and apartments. When I was little, several neat but tiny buildings went up where there used to be plum orchards and farm fields. They slapped fancy names on these—*Estates* or whatever—to help sell units. Nice-looking families moved in, and on weekends you'd see them out walking their dogs or driving around in expensive foreign cars. But the paved roads that run through the neighborhood, which must have been just dirt farm paths at one time, are so narrow that I heard the family two houses down from us had so much trouble parking their Mercedes-Benz in their garage that they ended up getting rid of it.

The siren keeps on droning. Right in between one of its groans, I hear a loud sound, something breaking next door. Our houses are so close that if you open the window, you can hear the parents yelling at each other, or the phone ringing. I'm thinking maybe a

3

window broke. Seven years ago the boy who lives in the house diagonally across from us kicked a soccer ball that shattered a window in our house in the room where we keep our Buddhist altar. The kid completely ignored what happened, and later on he was transferred to a school in Kansai. I remember the abandoned soccer ball sitting there under the eaves of my house forever.

Anyway, the sound I'd heard was just like that time. There aren't any little kids living next door, so it's weird to hear something shatter so loudly, and the whole thing was kind of alarming. Maybe a burglar broke in. My heart beating like mad, I listened carefully but didn't hear anything else. Total silence.

The neighbors moved in two years ago. We've had hardly anything to do with them. Sometimes, when I take the neighborhood association bulletin to them, I'll press the intercom bell and the mother will come out, this phony smile pasted on her face. All I know for sure is that there's a mom and a dad, and a boy the same age as me who lives there. Sometimes the mother is out front, sweeping with a bamboo broom. She has on silver-framed glasses and this bright red lipstick you know is going to leave marks on any teacup she uses. Get rid of the glasses and the lipstick, though, and I don't think I'd recognize her.

Once when the woman next door saw me in my school uniform she asked, "Are you a high school student?" When I said yes, she said, "So is our son," and named the prestigious high school he attended, smiling happily. When I told my mom this, she clicked her tongue and looked disgusted. The woman was obviously bragging about her son and Mom must have thought she was insulting us, since I was going to a less-than-stellar private girls' school. But I just thought the woman next door was simple and naive, and I felt sorry for the boy for having such an embarrassing mother.

This son of hers was a lanky, stoop-shouldered boy with small, gloomy eyes. Reminded me of a worm. He had a sluggish way of walking with his head tilted to one side, and zero in the way of spirit. Even when our paths happened to cross at the station he'd avoid looking at me and edge off into the shadows of the building. Like if he stepped into the shadows he could hide from the world. In that sense he was just like his father, who looked like a typical office worker. The father ignored me as if I didn't even exist. Once I went out to get the evening paper when he was just coming home. I nodded to him but he gazed off into the distance like I was invisible.

"I wonder what that guy does for a living, anyway," my mother once said. "Kind of stuck-up with that ascot of his." Who cares about ascot ties? was my reaction. To me people are divided into two groups: the nice and the un-nice. And the family next door was definitely in the second category. If my grandmother were still alive she would have sniffed out all kinds of gossip about them, but my mother couldn't be bothered, so the only details we knew about them were that their son looked like a worm, the mother wore red lipstick, and the father, an ascot.

Still, I couldn't figure out what that sound was. A burglar could break into their house for all I cared, but I didn't want him coming into ours. I started to panic. My parents were both at work, I had slept in late and was about to have some cup ramen before heading out to summer cram school—I was a senior in high school—and the last thing I wanted was for some burglar to flee into our place. Dad always said that the scariest thing was a thief who gets cornered and turns violent.

I heard another crash, this one louder than the first. It rang in my ears, and I flinched and messed up my left eyebrow. Maybe I should redo it, I was thinking, staring into the mirror, when my cell phone on the table buzzed.

"Yo!" It could only be Terauchi. "Dude, it's me."

"I just heard this weird sound from next door—maybe a robber or something. What should I do?"

But Terauchi wasn't paying any attention.

"That essay on Mori Ogai we're supposed to write? I've done over a hundred pages, right? Just kidding . . . But I think it's going to turn out okay, know what I mean?" She rambled on like this for a minute or so.

"Terauchi. *Listen* to me. A burglar might have broken into the house next door."

"Duuuude!" Terauchi was finally surprised and her usual greeting now turned into an interjection. Terauchi was a cute-looking girl, but her voice was really low and cool. Among my friends, she was the smartest and the most interesting.

"I just heard glass shattering," I said. "Someone breaking in, maybe."

"Probably just the husband and wife having a fight."

"At this time of the morning?" I said. "The guy next door should be at work."

"Well, maybe the wife lost it and smashed a teacup or something. It's gotta be that," she declared. "You know, one time when my mom got into a fight with my dad's mother she went nuts and tossed both of their teacups and plates out the second-story window."

"Your mom's kind of extreme."

"You got that right," Terauchi said. "She just casually tossed the plates and cups out, aiming at the stepping-stones in the garden. See, Dad was using the plates Yukinari used as a baby. Anyway, Toshi-chan, I wanted to see how you're doing with your essay."

Toshi-chan. My name's Toshiko Yamanaka, the characters for *Toshi* meaning "ten and four," because I was born on the fourth

day of the tenth month, October. Obviously not a lot of thought
went into naming me, but since I've hardly ever met anyone with
the same characters, I don't mind the name that much. Terauchi's
first name is Kazuko, which she can't stand. Her grandfather in
Akita gave her the name, apparently. My friends all call one another
by their first names or by nicknames, except for Terauchi, who
insists that we call her by her last name.

"The thing is, I haven't done it yet," I admitted.

When we got to be seniors our Japanese teacher assigned us to
write an essay on Ogai's story "The Dancing Girl." Terauchi was
always good at exams and assignments. Whenever we had to write
a book report, she copied parts of some published essay on the
book without the teachers ever catching on. I was a little too
honest—honest to a fault, you could say—to try to get away with
something like that. So unfortunately it took me a lot of time to fin-
ish up assignments and my grades were never as good as hers. I
never thought of what she did as dishonest; I was kind of vaguely
worried that someday her cleverness might really her get in trouble. I worried about her because I liked her so much.

She went on, rumbling in her low voice: "I was thinking of, like,
doing a psychological analysis of the main character."

"Including Elise?"

"Nah—not her. Her name's in katakana. What's his name—
Oda?"

I didn't have a clue what she was talking about.

"That's not it," a different voice replied. Now it was Yuzan on
the phone. "She's gonna do a psychological profile based on the
Chinese characters used to write the name. Can you imagine getting away with that?"

"Yuzan, I didn't know you were there," I said.

I must have sounded a little disappointed. I wasn't exactly

happy to find out that she and Terauchi were hanging out without me. It made me feel left out. I really liked Terauchi, but Yuzan was harder to deal with. She had such extreme likes and dislikes. She hated smokers violently, for instance. Human garbage, she said. Which was kind of unfair from the smoker's viewpoint. On the other hand, if she liked somebody she'd stand up for them, no matter what. Extreme and hard to read—that was Yuzan.

"Terauchi wanted to do homework together. I told her we're not in grade school anymore. Duh!"

"I bet that it was *your* idea," I countered.

Yuzan just laughed this off. Her voice was even lower than Terauchi's, and when she wore her school uniform she looked like some guy doing a lousy job of dressing in drag. Her personality and the way she spoke were totally like a guy; but her name, Kiyomi Kaibara, was very feminine. The nickname Yuzan, of course, came from Yuzan Kaibara, the father character in the manga *Oishinbo*. When she was in junior high, her mom died after a long stay in the hospital. Since then Yuzan's lived with her father and grandparents. Yuzan and I were only children, the only ones in our group. After her mother died, Yuzan started acting even more eccentric, even more like a guy. Terauchi said Yuzan must be a lesbian, but I couldn't really see it. Even if she were, I wouldn't know, I guess, because I wouldn't be her type. I switched the phone to my other hand and heard this sort of grabby sound as Terauchi came back on.

"That's the story, dude."

"Fine, whatever—but should I just ignore what's going on next door?" I asked.

"That's their business, not yours. Don't you think so?"

Terauchi's cool reply made me feel better. "I guess you're right," I said. "Well. I gotta go to cram school. Talk to you later."

"See ya," she said, and hung up. I switched off the AC and checked my left eyebrow in the mirror again. I didn't like what I saw, but didn't have time to redo it, so I set off. I was wearing jeans and a black sleeveless shirt. A nothing sort of look, but something I felt comfortable in.

It was blindingly hot outside. I slipped on the new sandals I'd bought at the bargain shoe store that was a two-minute walk from our house, and unlocked my bike, which I'd left next to the front door. The handlebars and seat had baked in the sun and my hand sizzled when I touched them. Just then the front door of our neighbors' house slammed shut and their front gate creaked open. Someone was coming out. Anxious, but curious, I turned around. It was Worm, dressed in jeans and a navy blue T-shirt. There was a tiny white Nike swoosh on the chest of his shirt. He was carrying a black backpack I remembered seeing before. Thank God. It wasn't a burglar after all. He'd been at home. Relieved, I looked at him and our eyes locked. He looked happy and excited somehow, like he was going off on a date. That kind of look didn't suit him, and I quickly turned away. It was a strange feeling, like I'd seen something I shouldn't have.

"Sure is hot."

This was the first time he'd even spoken to me. I nodded vaguely. So that's the kind of guy Worm is. The kind who talks about the weather—and to somebody like me who's the same age. Humming a song, he squinted up at the sun. He looked so healthy that the nickname Worm no longer seemed right.

"I heard some loud sound from your house a few minutes ago and it startled me." I had to say something.

Still squinting up at the sky, he tilted his head. "Yeah? You must be mistaken."

"Sorry," I said.

Worm bounded off like he was heading off on a school outing. Embarrassed, I straddled my bike, shoved my bag into the front basket, and, without a glance backward, started pedaling toward the station. Soon I passed Worm, but I didn't say hi.

My cram school is near the south exit of a large station that connects up to the Chuo Line, four stops down the line from the station near my house. I was still thinking of Worm, actually about the sound I'd heard next door, and I got snagged by one of those people with clipboards asking you to fill out questionnaires. I'm usually careful enough to keep at least thirty yards between me and them, but this time I blew it. The questionnaire guy was dressed in a serious-looking outfit, white dress shirt and black pants, with the kind of black-framed glasses that are popular now.

"Are you a student?" he asked me.

"I'm in a hurry."

"It won't take long. You're in college?"

"That's right."

"A four-year college or community college?"

"Four-year. The education department at Tokyo University."

I stood there with this can't-be-bothered look on my face. The guy looked surprised for a second, then scribbled down "Tokyo University" in crappy handwriting. A sneer came to his face, like maybe he thought I was bragging. Or like he'd seen through my lie.

"May I ask your name?"

"Ninna Hori."

"How do you write it?"

"Hori is the character for 'moat,' and Ninna is written the same as the *ninna* in the Ninna Temple in Kyoto."

"The Ninna Temple?" the man muttered, and I used his moment of hesitation to make my escape. This was the first time I'd said I was a Tokyo University student. Usually I tell people I'm a secretary in an office, but with the crummy outfit I had on and my aggressive attitude, it seemed to fit. Whenever you have to write down your name and address for a questionnaire or membership form or at a store, it's best to use a phony name and address. Terauchi taught me that. The first time I did it I felt kind of nervous about lying, but after I'd used the name for a while, Ninna Hori started to feel like a real second name. In our four-girl group all of us have a second fake name that we used when we rented a karaoke box. You have to be careful, Terauchi always warned us, or you'll wind up in some database. Then adults will *control* you.

The next person who tried to grab me was a creepy-looking woman. As I sped up to get away, the woman, eager for the chance to interview someone, rushed forward and almost tripped up. She had a mound of black hair, chopped off in a bowl cut, and no makeup. Her upper lip was dripping sweat. White sweat stains showed in the armpits of her faded black blouse. It was steaming out, so I could hardly blame her for that, but it was so hot and uncomfortable all I could think of was shoving her out of the way.

"Excuse me," she said. "I'm studying fortune-telling and wondered if I could have a moment of your time?"

Fortune-tellers. They're all over the place. No way it's going to be free. I put on the impassive face I practiced in the mirror. "I'm in a hurry," I said.

"Pardon me." At seeing my determined face, the fortune-teller turned away and started wandering around for her next victim. It's not easy for a young girl to get past the crowds outside of a station without something happening. When I mentioned this to my mother, she sighed and said, "It wasn't like that in my day. So many dangers out there now." She's got that right. In Tokyo today young girls are seen as either easy marks for sales or as "marketing leaders" to help companies get a grasp on what new products are going to sell. They want to get our opinions for free. Which makes us another kind of easy mark, I guess.

Not to mention all the stalkers and perverts, all the horny men, both young and old, who call out, "Hey, babe, how much?" I've never actually run into perverts myself, but there's a rumor that Terauchi's had problems with them since she was in elementary school—she's run into them on the train commuting to school. Terauchi's so unique, almost scary smart, but since she's also pretty, everyone from adults to college guys underestimates her and makes a move on her. I figure these perverts are the reason she shows no interest in men, and why she sometimes has this gloomy look on her face, talks the way she does, and gets all depressed. Let's face it: the world is twisted. And rotten.

I rushed into the classroom in my cram school, the one for English for Top-Tier Private Colleges. I was a little late and in a hurry. The school had a rule that if you're late they won't let you in.

Four people who looked like college students, two guys and two girls, were standing in front of the blackboard, smiling at the students seated in front of them. I could tell at a glance they weren't teachers and weren't cram school students, either. Teachers are older and frumpier, students younger and less confident. Both the teachers and the students at this cram school lacked the same exact thing: affection for others. No room for that in a cram school. But these four guys and girls in front of us had these permanent smiles, as if they were the hot lifeblood that flowed through this cruel battleground. One of the girls, the collar of her white shirt pulled out over her gray power suit, spoke up:

"It's summer vacation already. Now's the time you've got to do your best and don't let yourself give up. There's still time. It's only the beginning of August. So no more complaining, just do the very best you can. If you don't, believe me—come next spring you won't be smiling. The spring when I became a senior in high school I was told to forget about getting into the university I was hoping for. It'll never happen, they told me. But, no exaggeration, that summer I spit up blood. I never worked so hard in my life. And I got into the Japan Academy of Arts. It gives you tremendous confidence, confidence that you can build on for the rest of your life. So I want you to give it everything you've got."

The girl paused, and gazed around the room.

"We're going to come around to each of you, so feel free to ask us anything."

The cram school had a system called My Tutor, which involved having college students hang around the classroom. They were supposed to be graduates of the cram school, but I wasn't buying it. During our short breaks they'd go around the classrooms, giving us little pep talks. The point being that having real-life college students among us was supposed to get us focused on taking entrance exams. Cheer us up. To me, though, they looked like Disney dolls, with toothy pasted-on smiles. I'd just barely slipped into my seat when the power-suit girl sidled over.

"You would be—Miss Yamanaka, correct?" the girl said, glancing at the list in her hand. "English isn't your subject, I take it. You have a fifty-two average. You've got to work harder if you expect to pass. Are you studying hard?"

It annoyed me to have everyone hear my average.

"My name is Ninna Hori."

The girl looked suspicious.

"Are you registered for this class, Miss Hori?"

"Yes, I'm signed up."

Keeping a perfectly straight face, I put my electronic dictionary on top of the desk.

"Really? Hmm. That's strange." The girl was taken aback. "I'll have to get the right list. Which colleges are you hoping to get into?"

"Sophia, or Keio."

"Then you'll have to do better in English. What's your average?"

"About fifty-eight," I lied.

"You'll need to be at least five points higher than that," the girl said, gazing at me closely. I could see the contact lenses pasted to her slightly popped eyes. "Anyhow, don't give up. If you study like you're going to die, it'll work out. Vocabulary, vocabulary. Memorizing vocabulary's the only way."

What did she mean, study like you're going to die? She said she spit up blood, but is that for real? Is studying really worth dying for? I couldn't accept it, and I guess that was one of my weak points. One of the other tutors, a guy in a white shirt and tie, was standing next to the prematurely bald guy in the seat in front of me, patting him on the shoulder.

"You've got to get your average up a bit," he said. "I know you can do it."

The balding guy, embarrassed, gave some vaguely positive reply.

"I studied twelve hours a day and raised my average by ten points," the tutor said.

"Really?"

You study twelve hours a day and your average goes up only ten points? Overhearing their conversation despite myself, I got depressed. While this was happening, the girl who'd counseled me went over to the quiet girl who sits behind me. The whole charade was disgusting. This was no better than getting caught by somebody at the station shoving a questionnaire in your face or trying to read your fortune.

They smile like mad but inside they couldn't care less about me. They're in it for the money. Or out to pick up somebody. Unlike Terauchi, I've never been openly propositioned, but I can understand the feeling that you're being targeted. If you fall for their lines you'll lose money and wind up suffering. It's a little like how, unless you watch yourself and try to stay under the radar, you get bullied. The world laughs at losers. But does that mean the ones who target other people and bully them are okay? No way. But everybody seems to forget that.

The sense of danger we all feel is something my mother can't comprehend. My mom's generation still believes in beautiful things like justice and considering other people's feelings. My mom's forty-four and runs a home nursing service with a friend of hers. She goes out herself to people's homes, so she's interested in things like social welfare and problems related to the elderly. Coming from me it might sound weird, but she's a pretty nice person. She's smart and knows how to stand up for what's important. She's genuine, and what she says is almost always right on target.

Dad works for a software company, and though he's usually out drinking, he's serious and a good guy. But even a nice mom and dad like this can't really sense how their child's been assaulted by commercialism ever since she was little, how she's lived in fear of being eaten alive by the morons around her. They just don't get it.

Mom always lectures me about not being afraid of getting hurt, but all she can imagine is the kind of hurt she's experienced herself. She has no idea of the threats that surround kids these days, how much we're bullied, how much hurt this causes.

For instance, since we were little kids we've been exposed to calls from people trying to get us to hire tutors, or cram schools trying to get us to enroll after phony free counseling sessions. You think that's going to raise your GPA? No way. That's something you have to do on your own. Walk around Tokyo and all you see are people trying to sell you something. Tell them okay and before you know it you've bought something. Make the mistake of telling them your name and address and now you're on a mailing list. Some old guy pats you on the shoulder and before you know what hits you you're in a hotel room. Stalkers' victims, the ones they kill, are always women. When the media was going nuts over school-girls getting old guys to be their sugar daddies for sex, that was the time when high school girls like us had the highest price as commodities.

It sucks. It totally and absolutely sucks. That's why I became Ninna Hori. Otherwise I couldn't keep myself together, couldn't survive. It isn't much, but it's the least I can do to arm myself. All these thoughts went through my mind as I fanned myself with the thin little textbook.

I somehow managed to stay awake till the end of class. I looked for my cell phone, thinking I'd call up Terauchi for a random chat, but my phone wasn't in my bag. I was talking with Terauchi before I left the house, so maybe I left it on the table. I was disappointed, but I didn't worry about it. I joined the horde of students streaming down the hallway hurrying home, when somebody called out from behind me.

"Toshi-chan!"

It was Haru, who's in my class at school. She's in one of the few Barbie Girl groups at our school. Now that summer vacation was here she was even tanner than before, her hair dyed almost totally blond, her nails manicured an eye-catching white. She had on heavy blue eye shadow and oversize false eyelashes, plus a gaudy red spaghetti-strap dress with pink polka dots. We used to be pretty good friends back in junior high, before she became a Barbie. Our freshman year of high school she even invited me to go karaoke singing with some college students.

"You came all the way from Hachioji?" I asked.

"I did," she said, fingering the strap of her cell phone with those nails that weren't what you'd expect to find on a student studying for college entrance exams. "The Kakomon Master Course here's supposed to be pretty good."

A fat boy from our cram school walked by, sweat dripping from his forehead, and openly sneered at Haru. You idiot, I thought. You have no idea how gutsy Haru really is.

"I'm taking the composition and English classes in the Top-Tier section," I told her.

"Good luck," Haru said. "Catch you later!"

Haru teetered down the stairs of the cram school on her platform sandals. The guys in the cram school made way for her. Like a timid queen, she stealthily walked down the middle of the stairs, and when she got to the landing, she waved to me. Like the fake names my friends and I use, Haru's disguise is her weapon. By becoming a Kogyaru or Yamamba or whatever they're called, I think Haru found a place where she could be totally accepted. Barbie Girls, Haru included, go to tanning places to get ultraviolet rays so their skin turns light brown, use oil pens for eyeliners, and glue on their eyelashes so they're permanently curled up. They're the ones who, more than anyone else, play around with their bodies.

My second weak point is that I feel put off by those kinds of outrageous outfits and makeup. Me, I just want to wear ordinary clothes and not stand out.

• • •

My face was dripping sweat. In the bicycle parking lot my bike was nowhere to be seen. It must have been stolen. It wasn't much of a bike, so why, of all the bikes in the world, steal mine? It was locked, too. I ran all around the huge parking lot, but no luck. Hot and angry, I ducked into a convenience store to cool off. I bought a plastic bottle of oolong tea and set off down the steamy road. In the twelve minutes it took to walk from the station my sandals gave me a terrible blister. Pissed off, I finally arrived home. The second-story window of the house next door reflected the orangish setting sun. Strange, I thought, none of the windows seemed broken. I remembered that sound I'd heard earlier and stood there, puzzled. I got the evening paper from the mailbox, held the cool bottle of tea to my burning forehead, and gazed again at the neighbors' house. The sliding doors to the Japanese-style room on the first floor were half open. Which was kind of weird, since the woman next door was such a stickler for keeping the place neat. Her windows always sparkled, and there was never as much as a single piece of litter in front of her house. Whatever, I thought, dying of thirst. I stepped inside my saunalike house, switched on the AC units in all the rooms, and drank down the oolong tea in a single gulp.

I rinsed out the empty tea bottle and tossed it in the recycling bin as I glanced at the table and realized my cell phone wasn't there. I must have taken it with me and dropped it. I calmly reviewed what I'd done since leaving home. I'd taken the phone with me and put it in my bag when I got on the bike. Then I parked the bike at the parking lot, went to cram school, and attended two classes. That's when I noticed the phone was missing, so I must have dropped it at either the station or the school. Or else it fell down into the bicycle's basket. I called the cram school and asked if anyone had turned in a cell phone, but they curtly told me no. I tried calling my cell phone number, but nobody answered. My bike and my phone. This sucks. I was beat, so I trudged upstairs to my sweltering room, flopped down on the bed, set the AC to high, and closed my eyes.

I dozed off until seven p.m. I heard the siren of a patrol car or an ambulance, but it just stopped nearby. The way it stopped all of a sudden was a little alarming, but I didn't worry about it. There's a chronically sick old person living nearby, so ambulances are often driving down our narrow lane. I couldn't sit around thinking about that. Mom would be home soon and I had to close the shutters and get the bath ready. I could imagine her unhappy tone of voice if she found out I didn't do any of my chores, so I dragged myself out of bed. Right then our phone rang.

"Dude."

"Terauchi, I lost my cell phone."

"Yeah, I called you and this weird guy answered."

"What kind of guy?"

"A young guy. When I said, 'Dude,' he yelled, 'Stop joking, you dummy.' Totally pissed me off."

I told her how I'd lost my cell phone and how my bike got stolen.

"He must have got your cell phone from the bike. You should get the service cut off right away. Forget about your bike, or else try to steal it back."

She was right. I hung up and ran downstairs, thinking I'd call and get the phone service cut off. The whole thing made me angry. All of a sudden I heard the rattle of a key and the door swept open. It was my mother. She had on white pants and one of my old blue T-shirts, and the basket-type bag she likes to carry around in the summer slung over her shoulder. She didn't have on any makeup and her face was sweaty and flushed.

"Oh, you're here. Thank goodness!"

She looked relieved. But she also looked pale and upset.

"What's going on?" I asked.

"You don't know? There's a police car outside the neighbors'. Apparently the woman next door was murdered. Her husband found her when he came back from work. I was so worried that something had happened to you, too."

Since morning I'd had this bad feeling, and now it felt strange that it had actually materialized into something. I felt like bragging to everybody about what a great sixth sense I have.

"The police said they'll be over soon to talk to us. How frightening! How could something like this happen? And in our neighborhood. What should we do? Should we call your father? I guess we'd better let him know."

Mom always kept her cool but now she was definitely flustered. I sat down on the sofa in the living room and started to think about the bad feeling I had when I heard the smog siren and then that crash came from next door. Was that the instant the woman was murdered? Could Worm have done it? I recalled how cheerful he seemed as he hummed and gazed up at the sun.

"Toshiko, the police want to talk with you."

I looked up and there at the front door stood an elderly man in a white polo shirt and a middle-aged woman in a black suit, both of them gazing into our house. I didn't like the look in their eyes. That's when I decided not to tell them anything about what I'd seen and heard.

Their questions seemed endless. I told them that I left the house to go to cram school about twelve, and didn't hear anything or see anybody. Their questions implied that they thought it was right about that time that the woman was killed. In other words, it looked like my testimony was key. One final question, they said. It was obvious that the police were suspicious of Worm.

"Have you seen the boy next door today?"

"No," I said.

I pictured Worm's expression. His happy, excited face. What was that all about? Did he feel liberated by killing his mother? Or was he just plain crazy? I wasn't so much afraid of him as curious to know what he'd been thinking. I was sure that he would never tell adults how he felt then. Maybe he wouldn't even know how to explain it. Or else if he tried, it would be so simple he'd hesitate to go into it. I think I know how he feels. Probably he just felt his mother was a pain. A real pain. If you told adults that was the reason you killed your mother, they wouldn't believe you. But it's the truth. The whole world's a pain. Such a pain, you can't believe it. Still, freaking out over it like he did was stupid. When high school girls like us freak out, people are always able to overpower us before we do something stupid, like hijacking a bus or running around with a knife. Which is why girls arm themselves beforehand so they don't get caught up in something like that. Boys probably aren't so good at protecting themselves.

"Were you friends with the boy next door?"

"Not at all. We didn't even say hi when we ran into each other. It's like we're, you know, strangers. Like we're living in two different worlds."

"Different worlds? How so?" asked the female detective in the black suit. She had on white sunblock makeup and her hair was done up, like when you wear a kimono. It was tied back by this girlish hair tie made of red and purple ribbon with millions of tiny flowers on it. She looked kind of silly, but her eyes were sharp, like she was seeing right through my lies. I got nervous, sure that she would figure out I was lying.

"I don't know," I said.

I didn't want to know anything about Worm's world. I live in a world where I think I'm right, a world that frightens me, and not since I was little was I naive enough to think that other people's worlds were the same as mine. When I did once blurt out that everybody must agree with me on this, I caught hell for it. People won't stand for others being different from them. Since I'm a little different from other people, I learned this early on. At school people form little four-five person cliques, but I never wanted to be with them or get to know them. Actually, I wasn't able to. In my class there are all kinds of people—Barbie Girls like Haru, nerds, and kids that fall into easy-to-classify groups because they're in clubs. Fortunately for me, I ran across some girls I could get along with so I could enjoy high school life okay, but it must be awful for kids who don't get along with anybody. We're different from our parents, a completely different species from our teachers. And kids who are one grade apart from you are in a different world altogether. In other words, we're basically surrounded by enemies and have to make it on our own.

"Tell me, since you're both in high school, how does the neighbors' boy strike you?"

"What do you mean?"

"Is he handsome, or the type who's popular with girls?"

The female detective smiled, and I could see her white overlapping teeth through her bright red lips. Lipstick was smeared on her teeth. I remembered the woman next door with her bright red lipstick, and though I didn't have any feelings for her one way or the other, I suddenly got frightened thinking that Worm had murdered her. I couldn't figure out why he'd do something like that, and it gave me a weird, spooky feeling. I was sitting there staring into space when the female detective rested her hand on my knee.

"Well?" she said.

It felt hot and awful to have someone else's hand on me like that, and I shifted to the side so her hand slipped off my jeans.

"To tell you the truth . . ."

"Please, go right ahead. He's the victim's son, so there's no need to hold back. We'll forget we heard it from you."

If you're going to forget it, then why even ask? I thought. But my mom was watching me with a worried frown, and the older detective looked all serious as he was scribbling notes, so I went ahead and told them.

"Well, he's kind of gross," I said. "Nerdy, and sort of gloomy, like you never can figure out what he's thinking. Like a withdrawn loner who just studies hard all the time."

A withdrawn loner who just studies hard all the time. That seemed to strike a chord. The two detectives shared a glance and stood up. My words seemed to make them label Worm a typical nerdy guy from a family that pushed its kid too hard to succeed in school—so he flipped out.

They questioned my mom, too, as she sat there at one end of the sofa. What kind of woman was the lady next door? How did the family seem to get along with each other? Any hint of domestic violence? I noticed that even before they began, the police had a set pattern of questions. It was after nine p.m. when they finally finished. All the lights were on next door, so they must still have been combing the place for evidence. I could picture Worm's father, in shock, leading the police from room to room. I let out a deep sigh. He'd always treated me like I didn't exist, but still it seemed outrageous for this to happen to him.

"This is terrible," my mother said. "The police haven't said anything but it's pretty obvious they suspect the son. They told me the father's a doctor who works in a hospital. We're neighbors and yet I didn't even know that. I wonder if they forced their son to study all the time to get into med school."

I was looking at the TV guide in the evening paper and didn't reply.

"How can you be so easygoing at a time like this?" my mother suddenly yelled at me.

"It doesn't have anything to do with us," I said.

"True, but you knew the lady next door, didn't you? And now she's dead. Whether the son did it or not, I feel sorry for him and the mother. I even feel sorry for the father, that stuck-up man with the ascot. His own son killed his wife, can you imagine? How could they ignore things until it came to this?"

"So what?"

I don't know why I lashed out at her. What she said made sense, but something just wasn't right about it, which really bothered me.

"You shouldn't talk like that," my mom said.

Her eyes were fixed. The front door opened and Dad came in. He had on a crummy light brown jacket and a black briefcase under his arm. His navy blue polo shirt was all sweaty. His eyes had the same fearful look as Mom's. She must have called him and he'd rushed home. He always says he's busy, but if he needs to he can come home right away. He turned to Mom first.

"Man, what a shock," he said. "The police just questioned me outside. I didn't know anything. They were amazed when I told them I didn't even know they had a son the same age as Toshiko."

Mom looked at him with this look that said, You're always out drinking and never come home, that's why. The whole thing was too much, so I tossed the newspaper on the table and was about to go upstairs to my room. Dad looked over reproachfully at the scattered paper.

"Toshiko. What happened to your bike? It's not outside."

"Yeah, what happened was . . . I parked it in the parking lot at the station but it got stolen."

"Why don't you report it? The place is swarming with cops."

Dad chuckled at his little joke but soon turned serious.

"It's okay," I said. "We wouldn't find it anyway. Sometimes people just use bikes and bring them back to the parking lot. Whoever took it will bring it back."

"I suppose you're right."

Dad didn't seem to care one way or another. *You're so careless!* Mom would normally have yelled at this point, but she was preoccupied, boiling noodles, slicing ham, preparing a late supper for us. As I walked up the stairs I could hear my parents talking, keeping their voices down so I couldn't catch anything. I stopped halfway up the stairs to eavesdrop.

"The inside of the house is apparently a wreck," Dad said. "The glass door to the bathroom was shattered when the woman was thrown against it, and she was covered in blood."

"I don't doubt it. They said her skull was bashed in by a baseball bat."

"What could possibly have made him do it?"

"He must have gone crazy. He took off his bloody T-shirt, they said, and put it in the laundry. He must have calmly changed his clothes and then gone out. I can't believe it—a wimpy little boy like that."

"Boys are strong," Dad said. "He might be skinny, but boys that age are stronger than you'd imagine. And they don't know how to control themselves. I'm sure glad we had a girl."

"What a terrible thing to say. That's kind of self-centered, don't you think?"

Chastened, my father said, "Guess you're right. Sorry."

• • •

I sat down on my bed and called my cell phone from my room phone. "Hi," a young guy answered. Damn, I thought. In the background I could hear the roar of trains going by. He was outside.

"You're the person who found my cell phone."

"I'm not sure if 'found' is the right word," he said.

The guy seemed hesitant. His voice sounded similar to the one that had said, "Sure is hot."

"Where did you find it?" I asked.

"In the bike basket."

Was this the person who stole my bike? My blood began to boil.

"Did you steal my bike?"

"Stole, or borrowed—I'm not sure how to put it."

"That's my phone and I want it back. If you don't return it you won't be able to use it anyway 'cause I'll stop the service. And I want you to give my bike back. I need it."

"I'm sorry," the guy apologized.

"One other thing. Are you the boy next door?"

All of a sudden the phone clicked off. I hit redial but he didn't pick up. I kept on calling, my knees shaking. I was starting to suspect that the guy who stole my cell phone and bicycle was Worm. Finally I left a message.

"This is Toshiko Yamanaka. I want you to return my cell phone and bike. My home phone number is under Home on the cell, so call me there. Between nine a.m. and noon I'm home alone, don't worry. Please call me. I'll tell you something else, 'cause I think you're the boy next door. The police are looking for you. I think you know why. It has nothing to do with me, but it was a shock to hear about your mother. I feel sorry for her. I probably won't say anything to them, but I don't really know what I should do."

I left this message on the phone, and felt depressed afterward.

That night I couldn't sleep well. I dozed off and had some weird dreams. The one I remember the most is this:

The woman next door was in my house, cooking dinner. Worm and I were in the living room, watching TV and laughing till tears were streaming down our faces. Worm and I were brother and sister, apparently, and the woman next door was our mother. Far away a smog alert siren sounded. Worm said, "It's hot, so let's have fried rice. . . . Fried rice sounds good." I went to the kitchen to wheedle the woman into making it for us. Mom, I said, make some fried rice for us, okay? The woman stared at me from behind her silver-framed glasses, then took out a wok and pointed at the bathroom. He pushed me against the door over there, she said, so I'm not going to cook for you. But Mom, the door to the bathroom isn't glass, so it's okay. There must be some mistake. It seemed to be a dream where I knew what Worm had done, but I was doing my best to calm her down anyway.

I woke up all sweaty and looked around my room trying to figure out where I was. It had been light out for some time, apparently. The sun had come up as always and a new day was beginning. It looked like it was going to be another hot one. Another day like all the others, but since yesterday morning my world had imploded. That crashing sound I heard when the smog alert sounded echoed over and over in my mind. I hadn't seen the bloody face of the woman next door, but I could imagine how awful it must have looked, her glasses flung aside. The dream I had must have been suggestive—telling me that I was knowingly aiding and abetting Worm after his "matricide." Maybe I'd be seen as an actual *accomplice* in the murder. The fact scared me silly. If Worm was caught, wouldn't they think that I'd lent him my phone and bike to help him get away? I suddenly felt like Worm had forced some awful thing into my hands. Now it had liquefied and was dripping down between my fingers. I was terrified—of the police, and the adult world. The warmth of the female detective's hand on my knee came back to me, and I shuddered.

I should have told my parents everything, before this got completely out of hand. I'd just about made up my mind when I heard Mom downstairs getting breakfast ready. She was grinding coffee beans. The same old world as always. Relieved, I got out of bed. My mom might have a different take on things than me, but at least she was a buffer between me and the police and the adult world. I was happy I had a mom and dad like that. Just then I heard voices outside, so I opened the window and peeked out. The narrow street outside our house was packed with people. People lugging TV cameras, newspaper reporters, a woman who looked like a reporter, and police. The reporter was from one of those TV tabloid shows. I ran downstairs.

"Good morning. You're up early." My mom, her face gaunt, was stirring eggs.

"Mom, did you see all those people outside?"

"They're from a tabloid show," my mother said, her face dark. "I hate having all these people crawling about. They must be hoping the son will come back home. How vulgar. I mean, they don't even know yet if he's the one who did it. And besides, he's a juvenile. All this racket's driving me crazy. Sorry, but could you go out and get the paper?"

I didn't have a bra on and was wearing a T-shirt and shorts I used for pajamas, but I said okay. I was curious to see how the papers were covering the incident and to see what the people from the TV tabloid show were like. As soon as I stepped outside, the hum of the people talking stopped cold. I was walking over to the newspaper box next to the front door when a woman reporter thrust a microphone in my face.

"Excuse me, I just have a couple of questions about the people next door. What sort of family were they?"

So this is a reporter? The other people stood there, holding their breath, waiting for my reply. Here I was, dressed like this, on national TV. I got all jittery and started inching backward, newspaper in hand. As soon as I reached the door I leaped inside. The tabloid show was on TV in our living room. Dad was sitting in front of the TV, his face swollen, chuckling to himself.

"Hey, you were just on TV."

The screen showed the road in front of our house with the caption "Live from the Scene" in white. You could see our house and the one next door, lit by the morning sun. It looked cramped yet showy at the same time. Ah, I thought, stunned, too late now. Now that it was such big news, I had to keep quiet about what I knew. That ominous sound, meeting Worm right afterward, the contented look on his face, the fact that he stole my bike and cell phone. I didn't think I'd be telling anybody about any of these things. The word *accomplice* ran through my mind again.

My dad folded up the newspaper and said, "I wonder why it happened. When I was young there were times I wanted to kill my old man and some of my teachers—but I never thought of killing my mom. It was like she was part of a totally different world from me. I never thought my mom was controlling my life or anything. Have you ever thought that?"

"Never."

Which was a lie. I think about it every time I fight with my mom, and there are tons of people I hate so much that I wouldn't mind taking them out. Even Terauchi and Yuzan—sometimes I hate them and want to kill them. But killing them wouldn't get me anywhere—that's the conclusion I always come to. If I'm going to have to pay for it in the end, I might as well let them live.

"The man next door apparently worked at the Kanto Fukagawa Hospital," Dad said. "In internal medicine. The poor guy. What was the son's name, anyway? It's not in the paper."

"Of course not. He's a juvenile," I said, depressed. Dad gulped down his coffee and exhaled, spewing coffee breath all over the place.

"I guess it'll be a big story for a while."

Mom called out from the kitchen: "Those people will be out there until the boy comes home. What should we do?"

"Just carry on as always," Dad said.

"If we could do that, there wouldn't be a problem."

"We'll just have to work around it. We're not involved."

But your daughter is! I wondered how astonished my dad would be if he knew that.

After my parents went to work I watched some of the tabloid shows on TV. They were all the same. *Is he involved in his mother's murder? The high school son vanished. Midsummer madness— what happened with this seventeen-year-old?* While I was watching TV we had two sets of visitors. The first was this middle-aged couple who said they were the older brother and sister-in-law of the man next door. We're so sorry to cause you all this trouble, they said, bowing and scraping like crazy, and handed me a heavy box of sweets. I opened it and found thirty *mizuyokan* sweets inside.

The second set of visitors were the detectives from the day

before. The old detective, wiping the sweat off with an oversize handkerchief, asked, "About the boy next door . . . we have a witness who saw him walking on the road to the station around noon yesterday. You told us you went to the station at about the same time. Didn't you see him?"

"I was riding my bike."

Damn! As soon as I said this I realized I shouldn't have. They'll find out my bike isn't there. Unconsciously I looked down.

"Didn't you overtake him on your bike?"

The female detective asked this. This day she had on a white blouse and a heavy cloisonné brooch near her collar. Like yesterday, her hair was loosely done up. The color of her face and the skin of her neck were five degrees off. I shook my head.

"I didn't notice him," I said.

"Aren't you going to cram school today?"

"Yeah, I am."

The phone rang. The two detectives motioned for me to get it. Heart slamming in my chest, I went to answer it. For all I knew it might be Worm. Whoever was on the other end didn't respond.

"Hello? Hello?"

The two detectives, standing at the entrance, looked at me suspiciously. I looked away and just started talking.

"Oh, Terauchi? Did you see the TV show? Sorry to have worried you. We have some guests now so I'll call you back."

The person on the other end finally spoke.

"The cops are there, aren't they. I'll call back later."

It was Worm. I hung up like nothing was going on. This was like something out of a movie.

"Sorry to keep you waiting."

I went back to the two detectives. The man, apparently farsighted, was squinting at his notebook. "The person who saw the

young man stated that he was wearing a navy blue T-shirt and
jeans," he said, "and was carrying a black backpack. The person
who saw him was a housewife who lives behind your house. She
was pushing her baby in a stroller to a park nearby. She said she
passes in front of the boy's house every time she goes to the station, so she's seen him a number of times. This housewife also said
that she saw someone who looked like you pass her by on a bike.
Are you positive you didn't see him?"

"Really? Well, it must have been just around twelve, because I
took the 12:05 express." I looked casual as I said this, and the two
of them wrote it all down. I'm glad I didn't have to lie about that.
Facts pile up like this, one after another. They'd find out soon
enough that Worm had broken the lock on my bike and stolen it.

"If anything changes, or you remember anything else, please
call this number. We'll be coming every day, so if you'd like, you
can tell us later."

The female detective handed me her card, which had rounded
edges, and I mumbled a word of thanks. After they left I felt on
edge. The phone rang again, and thinking it might be Worm, I
answered in a low voice.

"Toshi-chan—is that you? What's the matter? You sound upset."

The voice was the opposite of Terauchi's—clear and bouncy.
This was my friend who went by the nickname Kirarin. Me, Terauchi, Kirarin, and Yuzan. This was the group I was in throughout
junior and senior high. Kirarin's real name was kind of odd—Kirari
Higashiyama—and even though she didn't like it, we all called her
Kirarin. She was cute, cheerful, a well-brought-up, proper young
girl. The name Kirarin was perfect for her, and she was the only
one in our group who could fit in nicely wherever she went.

"You lost your cell, didn't you, Toshi? Last night the guy who
picked it up called me."

"What time was it?"

"About ten maybe?" Kirarin said lightly. "I went to a movie and was on the train back when he called. I couldn't really talk a lot, but it was fun and I ended up talking about all kinds of things. I'm sorry. I shouldn't have—the guy's got a lot of nerve."

I was so surprised I didn't know what to say. Kirarin went on. "I told him you need your cell phone and he's got to give it back. And he's like, Sorry, I understand, I'll definitely give it back."

"Apologizing to you isn't going to help. He's got to tell *me* he's sorry."

"Totally."

Kirarin laughed cheerfully. Come to think of it, she's the only one of my friends I've never felt like killing. It's like I was always praying that she'd stay as cute as she was and always be the one who smoothed things over among us.

"But hey—why aren't you in cram school?" she asked.

"I'll tell you about that later. I gotta go. I've got to ask Yuzan if she got a call, too."

"Let's all get together during summer vacation," Kirarin said. If Worm had phoned Kirarin he might have called Yuzan, too. Both their names were in my contacts list, so he was just having fun calling them at random. What a jerk. I called Yuzan right away.

"Yeah, hello . . ." Yuzan said, her voice low and cautious.

"It's me. Toshi."

"Hey, Toshi. There wasn't any caller ID, so I was wondering who it was. I heard you lost your cell phone?"

"The guy called you?"

"Yep. I thought it was you, but it was a guy. What a shock. We must have talked for thirty minutes."

I didn't know what to say. What could Worm have talked about for a half hour? And with my friend? It made me really angry—

I couldn't believe that she talked with him that long. This was the guy who killed his mother with a baseball bat! The guy who smashed her against a glass door! Who stole my bike and cell phone and ran away! It gave me the creeps how mellow he seemed about the whole thing. When I'd recovered enough to talk, my voice was sharp.

"Listen, Yuzan. How could you talk for a half hour with the guy who stole my phone?"

"Sorry. I know I shouldn't have done it. But you know, he's pretty funny. He was telling me all about killing his mother, so I told him I murdered my mom three years ago and he fell for it. Then we talked about exams and life, all kinds of things."

"But your mom was sick. That's why she died."

I must have sounded kind of depressed, because what happened to Yuzan's mother and what Worm did were so very different. Yuzan seemed upset and didn't say anything. Losing her mom hurt her more than any of us could imagine and we all knew never to bring up the subject. Here I was rubbing salt in her wound. So how could Worm, who killed his own mother, and Yuzan have so much to talk about? I felt like I'd taken on a stupid, even comical role because I knew everything that was going on and I felt so upset by the whole thing. It was so idiotic. I had no idea what to do.

"I'm really sorry, Yuzan. Anyway, I want him to give me back my bike and cell phone."

"Understood. I'm going to see him today, so I'll get them back."

"Where is he? I'll go with you."

"No, I can't tell you. I promised." Yuzan clammed up. I couldn't stand it anymore, so I told her everything that had happened since the day before. She listened without saying a word.

"So what's the problem?" she said. "It's not our business. Worm killing his mother has nothing to do with us."

"I know," I said, angry. "I don't care about that at all. I just want my bike and my phone back."

"Okay. I'll make sure he gives them back."

The phone clicked off. As I set it down, all sticky after talking so long, I thought, Damn! I happened to see a headline in the paper: "Housewife Murdered in Broad Daylight." The article didn't mention the missing son much, but anybody reading it would see that he was under suspicion: "The son's bloody shirt was tossed into the laundry basket, and the police are searching for the boy in order to question him about the incident." The incident? I couldn't care less about that. I just wanted my bike and phone back. Behind this, though, a thought weighed heavily on me, namely that Worm had talked so much with Kirarin and Yuzan, not me or Terauchi. In other words, he didn't think either I or Terauchi was worth talking to. I got irritated, realizing that I felt Worm had betrayed me. I mean, who cares about him, anyway?

The smog alert groaned out again. I was wondering why I didn't hear that woman's usual languid announcement, so I looked outside. There were even more reporters than before, all sweating and staring at the house next door. A random thought occurred to me. There aren't any hidden speakers for the smog alert. They must use a PR truck that drives around and makes the announcements.

That night, around ten, the doorbell rang. Mom had just taken a bath and, thinking it might be the police again, she frowned as she went to the front door.

"Toshiko, it's Kiyomi. A little late, don't you think?"

"I know, but she's got something she's got to tell me."

"It's hot out, so have her come inside."

Mom was taking out some cold barley tea from the fridge as she said this, a dubious look on her face. Dad was still out late, as always. One day after the shocking murder and he was back to his old routine. I went outside and was hit by the stifling, muggy air. I could feel the moisture on my AC-cooled skin grow sticky. There weren't any reporters now, and the road was deserted. Yuzan was standing in front of our gate, holding my bike. She had on a T-shirt and Adidas shorts, Nike sandals and a backpack. If you saw her from far away you might take her for a short high school boy. She was huffing and puffing so much she must have ridden all the way here.

"Sorry to come so late," she said, out of breath.

"It's okay. Thanks for bringing it."

I put the bike inside our gate. As I did, my arm rubbed against Yuzan's bare arm. Her arm was all sweaty. Startled, I pulled away and our eyes met.

"Is that the guy's house over there?" Yuzan motioned with her chin. Worm's house was dark and still. Until last night the place had been crawling with investigators, but now it was deserted, like a discarded, empty shell.

"Yeah, that's it. I think his room's on the corner there, on the second floor."

I pointed to the pitch-black window. Yuzan gazed at it for a while, then sighed and looked away.

"Yuzan, where did you guys meet up?"

"In Tachikawa. It sure was a long way to come here."

"What's he doing in Tachikawa?"

Yuzan took out a plastic water bottle from her pack and took a drink.

"He says he's hiding out in a park there. Said he used to swim in the pool there when he was little. Said he used to have a good time, so he wanted to see the place again. He must have spent the day hanging out around the pool, 'cause he's totally tanned."

I tried to imagine Worm at the pool with his mom wearing her silver-framed glasses, and his dad with his ascot, but I just couldn't picture the three of them together like that.

"What'd he say?"

Yuzan screwed the cap back on her water bottle. "Said he feels like he's in a dream. Like the past, too, is all a dream." She gazed back up at the empty house and I decided to go ahead and ask her something: "Did you feel the same way about your mother?"

"Um." Yuzan nodded. "Sometimes I can't even believe she ever existed."

Yuzan and Worm shared this emotion, I could tell, something I would never be a part of. This didn't make me sad exactly—it was more a feeling that my own world was too simple, too smooth, too boring and worthless. The most I could do was have another name, Ninna Hori.

"Oh, I've got something for you. He told me to say he's sorry."

She carefully extracted my cell phone from a pocket of her backpack. I switched it on and found that the battery was almost dead.

"Well, gotta run," she said.

Yuzan started walking off toward the station.

"What did he say he's going to do? Keep on running?"

"Yeah. I gave him my own bike and cell phone, so he says he's going to run as far as he can."

I looked at Yuzan, astonished. She passed by me and stared up again at the deserted house next door. I stood there, clutching my cell phone, wondering if Worm would get in touch, suddenly realizing I was hoping he would. I didn't want to be an accomplice, but I did want a taste of adventure, like what Yuzan was doing. Kind of a lame attitude, I know, but that's the way I am sometimes. That realization put me in a gloomy mood for the rest of the night.

I can still picture Toshi's surprised look. She was in shock about the woman next door getting murdered, plus her bike and cell phone being stolen. I'm sure she never imagined I'd help out Worm that much. Well—I guess I'm pretty surprised myself.

Toshi acts all laid-back and careless, but she's built a Great Wall around her heart. It looks like you can get inside but it's not easy. That's 'cause she's much more fragile than other people. She's been hurt a lot in the past. But that's what I like about her. She's timid, but she manages to take care of herself. I think she's actually the toughest out of the four of us. So when I told her about what I'd done and she gave me this sort of what-are-you-talking-about look, I felt uneasy. Like because of this whole incident I've been expelled to some universe far away from the world Toshi lives in. It's not like I feel alienated from her or anything. It's more like from this point on, the two of us were going to walk down very different paths.

With all these worries running through my head, I hurried down the dark road. The neighborhood was quiet. I was afraid there might be cops staking out Worm's house, but there were only a few office types coming from the station. The trees that hung over the road gave off a heavy dampness, like when rain has just let up. The ground was still midsummer hot, and I felt like my body was slicing through the wet air.

In earth sciences class we learned that only fifty percent of the sun's energy reaches the surface of the earth. Our teacher printed up two graphs on his computer to explain it to us. "This one's the breast of a young woman, this one, that of an old granny," he explained, a serious look on his face. The young woman graph was supposed to show how the heat energy accumulates a lot around the equator, while the old woman graph was flat and showed solar energy radiating away. How dumb can you get, I thought, but there were only five of us in the class so we all had to pretend it was funny. The teacher himself said that explaining things like that might constitute sexual harassment. Like I cared. What a loser.

He went on, saying, "At the equator the amount of heat absorbed is more than the heat radiated away, so it's a heat source. The polar regions are the opposite—they're cold sources." A *cold source*. The vague thought crossed my mind then that that's exactly what I'd been back then. By *then* I mean my mom's death and one other thing that happened. I was just radiating away heat, like the poles, and in my whole life I'd never be warm. That made me sad, and I got depressed.

Toshi, Terauchi, and Kirarin all have both parents and pretty affluent families, and I doubt whether they have the kind of worries I have. After my mother died I was left with my pain-in-the-butt dad, and grandparents who worry over everything. I doubt they have any idea how I really feel.

Sometimes my friends will start to say something about their mothers, then notice my expression and get all flustered. Before this happens, though, I try to say something, something stupid like my teacher said. Or even dumber. Or else fill in the gap by asking something about *their* mothers, like, "Hey, Kirarin, is your mom coming to the school festival or what?" Is there any other high school student who has to be walking on ice like this all the time? What a joke.

I feel so alone. And there's a good reason for this. Mom's death only made me lonelier, lonelier than anybody. Worm felt a little lonely and killed his mom, perfecting his solitude. I don't know how I'm going to do it, but I want to perfect mine, too. Maybe life would be easier then. I've only talked about this with Terauchi—not because she's so gloomy, but because her gloominess and mine are similar. Toshi and Kirarin are too gentle and kind to talk to about this. I figure being gentle means you must be happy. Terauchi, though, is more edgy. I like the edgy, risky types, and feel closer to her. But I haven't told her yet about Worm. I'm not sure why.

The cell phone in my pack buzzed against my back. I stopped, took it out, and saw that I had a text message.

> Thanks for the bike and phone. I've come to Iruma,
> but got tired so I stopped at a convenience store. I'll
> rest for an hour and then take off again.

It was from Worm. I lied when I told Toshi I'd given Worm my cell phone. She'll find out someday, but she looked so astonished I couldn't tell her the truth. Actually, I bought him a new cell phone. But lending him my bike—that part's true. Don't worry about it, I told him, you can get rid of it anytime you like. Otherwise people will find out I helped him.

I was thinking I'd phone Worm, and glanced at my watch. It was past ten fifteen p.m. I had to get back home or Dad would have a fit. Ever since that incident last summer, he's started to meddle in everything I do. I keep telling myself just to hang in there until I graduate from high school. I figured I'd call Worm after I got home, so for the time being I sent him a text message.

> I gave the phone and bike back to Toshi. Call her to
> apologize, okay? Take care of yourself.

I stared at the message. I was helping a guy escape—a guy who had killed his mother. I have no idea what made him do it, but I wanted him to run away and never get caught. I don't really know how to put it, but it was like I didn't want him to come back to stupid, boring reality, but instead create a new reality all his own.

I heard this sticky sound of footsteps like something being crushed underfoot, and I shoved my cell phone into my pocket. The tip of a cigarette glowed in the dark like a firefly. I was a little tense but then saw that it was just a young office-type girl in mule sandals. The weird sound as she walked came from her bare feet sticking, then unpeeling, from the sandals. As the girl passed by me, she flicked her cigarette butt aside. My nose was hit by the strong stink of nicotine.

"Don't throw your butt away like that!"

I said this without thinking and the woman turned around and glared at me. She was a hefty girl, about five-seven. She had on green phosphorescent eye shadow, and a blue camisole that barely fit her broad shoulders. One of your sulky, penniless Office Ladies. She looked like an unpopular, down-on-his luck transvestite. I suddenly remembered the shock I felt last year when a transvestite in the Shinjuku 2-chōme entertainment district roughed me up, and I held my breath.

"Don't preach to me, you bitch," the woman said in a shrill voice and briskly walked off. I stood stock-still under the streetlight and remembered that night last summer in Shinjuku, when I was in my second year of high school.

In the 2-chōme district there are several small bars that cater to only women.

I'd heard that the Bettina was the most radical, the one that turned away anyone who's straight.

I'd found it on the Internet and went to check out the place during summer vacation. I had a pretty good idea before I went what the bar would be like, but I just wanted to find out what sort of people went there. I guess I wanted to make sure I wasn't the only one who was like me.

The place was what I expected, a tiny, cheap bar that could seat barely ten people. The owner was a middle-aged woman who looked like a sushi chef—white shirt with the collar turned up, short neatly combed coarse hair with a sprinkling of gray. Most of the customers were disagreeable career hags on the lookout for young girls to snag. There were a couple of people like me who were curiously, nervously looking around. We all sported short haircuts, T-shirts, shorts, day packs, and sneakers—girls dressed just like your typical high school boy. They were junior and senior high school girls who had also found the bar on the Internet and had come to check it out during their summer break. The bar was well aware that summer vacation meant more junior and senior high school girls coming by, and they were nice enough to allow them to hang out till morning, like it was a onetime summer experience for them, for the price of a can of beer.

I got to know two girls there. One, named Boku-chan, had come to Tokyo from Kochi and was planning to stay as long as she could. The other, named Dahmer, was from Saitama, where she was a top student in an elite high school. All of us went by our pseudonyms, so it took a while before I learned their real names and where they came from.

Boku-chan was trying her best to become a guy. She was a dummy who thought that as long as she acted rough and squared her shoulders she'd look like a guy. Her dream was to make a living as a transvestite in the infamous Kabuki-chō district. She made it was obvious she was looking for a rich older woman. But really, age didn't matter—she'd have taken an elderly woman, someone middle-aged, or even a young hooker. Boku-chan had the simple fixed idea that, since she liked women, she wanted to become a nice man; and that in order to become one, she needed to act manly. Which to her meant frowning as you held your cigarette between thumb and forefinger, putting your arm around a girl's shoulder and lifting her chin with your finger, speaking in a deep, threatening voice, adopting all the poses and actions of hunky actors in movies. She was tall, had studied karate, and was muscular, so she had the mannerisms down, but somehow when she did it, it all came off as a joke. On top of that, she wasn't the brightest bulb in the box. Dahmer and I talked once about how if she actually did become a transvestite she'd run out of topics to talk about and customers would find her boring.

Boku-chan didn't have any money, so she slept on the street or hung out at Dahmer's, spending most nights during summer vacation in the 2-chōme district before she went home to Tosa Yamada in Kochi. My dad wouldn't allow her to stay in our house but that never seemed to bother her. Even now I get e-mails from her sometimes. Her e-mails are full of happy-go-lucky stuff like, *I just bought a purple suit in the shopping district. They had only a double-breasted one so I bought that, but I think single-breasted looks better on me.*

Dahmer, on the other hand, was a more complicated character, like me. She took her nickname from the serial killer in America. She was interested in cruel murders and dead bodies—kind of a death obsession. Since my mother died in the fall of my last year in junior high, I hate that kind of thing. I told Dahmer how I felt once, that people who are afraid of death and are the farthest from it are the most obsessed by it. She just shrugged. I think Dahmer felt the same kind of alienation from me that Toshi did when I told her about helping Worm. That was the only time we talked about death, and I never mentioned my mom again. I've packed away the pain so deep inside me that I can't even draw it out myself, and my body just continues to function like nothing had ever happened.

Dahmer's parents had gotten divorced and, like me, she was an only child. It was just her mom and her now, and her mom, she said, did all kinds of jobs and wasn't home very much. *That person*—that's how she referred to her mother. *That person's* fairly good-looking, she'd say. *That person's* a slacker. *That person's* got her own life to live. There was something similar about my mother's death and the way Dahmer referred to her mother. With both there's a sense of distance from the reality we live in. Like they're people who live in some far-off other country. No matter whether they're dead or alive.

Dahmer was in love with her female math teacher in high school. The woman was twenty-six, a graduate of a scientific university, a smart aleck who made fun of anyone who was less than a mathematical genius. Dahmer liked the woman's arrogance. She was always saying she wanted to be better than that woman, so she wouldn't be made fun of, otherwise she'd die. Once, when her grades fell below the class average, she got drunk and felt so humiliated she slashed her wrist with a knife. I saw it once, that thin scar on her arm. She was always lugging around a math textbook, but with Boku-chan hanging out at her place, she moaned and groaned about not being able to get much studying done. She loaned Boku-chan money, even let her borrow her T-shirts and shorts. If Boku-chan was too much for her, I figured she should just kick her out, but Dahmer was the type who couldn't say no. An idiot like Boku-chan was too much for her, but Dahmer had a weak point: she was also impressed by someone this dumb, knowing she couldn't act like that. Maybe this was the same sort of weakness that made her say that if people made fun of her, she'd die. I don't know.

I have my own weaknesses, and Dahmer and I share the same sense of despair, since we'd like to live a cool life but can't as long as we're burdened down with all these problems. I can't let on to my dad that I'm a lesbian, I can't seem to manage relations with people in high school, and I'm sure I'll never be able to do so. These are burdens I'll carry around the rest of my life. I get so scared thinking about the future it drives me crazy. Still, I just want my friends at school to think I'm a slightly mannish type of girl, nothing more, and I never, ever want the girls I'm friends with, Toshi, Kirarin, or Terauchi, to know that I'm a lesbian. Because of my issues, my life's pretty complicated and I feel constrained, like I have to keep a tight lid on who I really am.

I was happy to meet Dahmer, because I think she understood all that. I think she was the same way. On days when she didn't e-mail, I felt really down. Like lovers, we tried to tell each other what was going on every day. At the end of last year, though, I suddenly couldn't get in touch with her anymore. When I called her mother, she said, *"That person's* gone off to study in Canada. I'm sure once she settles in she'll e-mail you." Her voice was strangely high-pitched and cheerful. I thought it was funny that they both referred to each other the same way, but there was something odd about her mother's cheerfulness. I was wondering whether Dahmer had actually failed her math teacher by not getting her grades up and if she had died. I didn't ask anything more. And that was the last I heard of her.

The incident I keep mentioning took place at night, three days before the end of summer vacation. The same sort of muggy night as tonight.

Boku-chan had announced she was going home to Kochi, so the

three of us had a going-away party at Bettina. We had a few drinks but the party just didn't get going. We hardly said a word and avoided looking at one another. "This looks more like a funeral than a going-away party," the owner of the bar joked.

Boku-chan wound up spending a total of twenty-five days basically wandering around Tokyo. She hated getting all smelly sleeping on the streets, so the last half of her stay she slept over at Dahmer's, which made their relationship go from bad to worse. The reason being that Boku-chan was a slovenly "guy"—and she was also an impolite country hick. She'd sleep past noon, eat whatever she could find in Dahmer's fridge, leave the room a mess, and borrow Dahmer's clothes without asking. When she took a shower, she'd just leave it running forever and forget to put away the shampoo and soap. Dahmer typically did the cleaning and washing for her mom, as well as shopping for dinner, and she hit the roof. I think also, like me, she felt vaguely irritated and sad knowing that when this summer vacation was over, so was her childhood. We sat at the counter, sipping our beer and listening to Tracy Chapman singing "Fast Car." The owner liked the song but I thought it sucked.

"Man—this isn't what I expected when I said I'm going home," Boku-chan finally complained, but Dahmer and I kept quiet. We had long since gotten sick of this idiot.

"Next time I come I'm not getting in touch with you guys."

"Fine by me," Dahmer said, and glanced at her watch. "Almost time for the last train. I'm out of here."

Surprised, I looked up. Dahmer usually stayed out all night and took the first morning train home, but on this last night together she was acting cold. She whipped out her purse and paid. Her hair hung down on her forehead, but through it, her eyes were gloomy and grown-up-looking. Boku-chan shot Dahmer a quick glance and said, all smart-alecky, "Hey, Dahmer—guess you want to go back to being a straight-arrow high school student? No big deal, huh?"

"You got that right," Dahmer said lightly, and looked at me. "You want to, too, right?" Yep, I do, my look told her. And that was my honest intention. If I could be a self-respecting high school student again, then yes, that's what I wanted to be. But I knew that none of us could ever be an ordinary serious student again. Because we were girls who liked other girls. Boku-chan sat there, silent, toying with a box of Salem Lights.

"Well, Boku-chan. See ya. It was fun." Dahmer beamed at her and waved good-bye. Her slim white arm was girlish, and I watched it sadly.

"How cold can you get," Boku-chan grumbled, and, pushing off from the counter with both hands like some old guy, stood up. "I'm going out to drink by myself. Just can't take it otherwise."

I didn't feel like chasing after either of them, so I just sat at the counter. The owner stood there, unconcerned, a cigarette dangling from her lips as she scanned the jacket of a bossa nova CD. I waited until the trains weren't running anymore and left. This is the last time, I thought. I planned to walk all the way home from Shinjuku to my house, which was in Soshigaya in Setagaya-ku. I decided this would be the last time during summer vacation I'd come home at dawn and make my dad go ballistic. I still felt sorry for my old man for losing his wife, and I was trying my best to live up to his expectations. I felt relieved to have a made a friend like Dahmer, but having spent time with a trashy girl like Boku-chan made me disappointed in the whole 2-chōme scene. As I left the bar I felt I'd moved on in life, and then I felt both lonely and a bit proud of myself. I walked down the stairs and was heading down an alley when this huge woman abruptly stepped out from the shadows.

"Hey, you! C'mere."

It was a man's deep voice with a Kansai accent. He had on a black camisole and a formfitting tight white skirt. He had on ridiculously high silver mule sandals, and this made his whole body lean forward. His panty line was visible on his skirt. He had an oversize squarish butt, and a jet-black head of hair that was obviously a wig. Only his nails were gorgeous, painted with a green design. Overall he was a shabby, cheap transvestite. If you wonder why I remember all these details so clearly it's because the guy grabbed me by the sleeve of my T-shirt and wouldn't let me go, so I had time to take it all in.

"Whatya want?" I asked.

"You're kind of obnoxious, aren't ya?"

He smacked me next to my ear with a clenched fist, and my left ear went deaf. I started to fall to the ground but the transvestite held on tightly to my T-shirt and wouldn't let me fall as he continued to pound me.

"What're ya thinking, coming to a man's part of town like this? You're a woman, pretending to be some cool-looking guy, but you're the type who gives us a bad name. If you want a woman, leave it up to a man. You're an idiot. Just plain dumb. So it's okay for a guy to rough you up, don't ya think?"

The transvestite roughly grabbed my breast. No guy had ever touched me there before and it was a total shock.

"You got a pair like this yet you try to act like a guy. What a jerk! Bet you wish you had a cock, huh? You're worse than our crap. So go 'head and try some."

He pushed me onto a pile of garbage. My nose was bleeding, so

I couldn't smell anything. The owner of Bettina heard the commotion and ran out to help me. I was bleeding a lot, but not really hurt, and she thought she couldn't just leave me, since I was just a high school student, so she put me in a taxi. I was conscious but covered in dirt and blood as I stumbled into my house. My face was swollen for a while and I didn't go to school the first week of the second semester. When he saw me all beaten up, my father was dumbfounded, and was scared I'd been raped. He asked if somebody had done something to me. As I listened to his worried footsteps pacing around the house, I lay on the floor and laughed. It was something much worse than rape, Dad, what happened to your daughter. You have *no idea*.

I've never told anybody about this. I couldn't tell Toshi or Kirarin, or even Terauchi. Not even Boku-chan or Dahmer. I don't know why. I never set foot in the 2-chōme district again. It wasn't so much that I was afraid of the place itself, but I was afraid of the creatures who masqueraded as people. And I became afraid of myself for stirring up such hatred in others. I knew I liked girls and couldn't figure out who I was, yet that transvestite, grabbing my breasts, made me realize I'm also a woman. That summer I totally lost my confidence. Maybe that's why it wasn't such a shock when Dahmer suddenly disappeared.

It was exactly eleven when I got home. Dad was waiting outside for me, looking unhappy. He had on a loose-fitting green T-shirt, chino shorts, and Nike sandals, and was smoking. My old man is a freelance photographer. When Mom was still alive he was hardly ever at home, always out "on location," or so he said. But after she died he announced that he would work at his Tokyo studio. He didn't go out drinking so much, and never came home later than eleven. His income went down, which he complained about. To me this was a pain. I just wanted him to leave me alone, but ever since I got beat up he couldn't tell the difference between keeping an eye on me and standing guard.

"Hey, where's your bike?"

"I lent it to Toshi."

"How come?"

"Hers got stolen. It's just for the summer, so she can go to her cram school."

I slipped past him and went inside. Our Maltese, Teddy, ran over and started jumping on my legs. Teddy, my mom's dog, is our family treasure. I picked him up and started to go upstairs. I didn't see Grandpa and Grandma. They must have gone to sleep a long time before. Or maybe they were holding their breath, monitoring the conversation between me and Dad. Since they're my mom's parents they don't really care much about Dad. Their hopes and sympathies are all directed at me. Which is a royal pain, too, and kind of disgusting. Every night I said a little prayer that they might die soon.

"Toshi's the one who lives next door to the boy who killed his mother, right? You know him, don't you?"

Dad was obviously curious. He was the kind of guy who followed the news closely and picked up on things. I hated that, too.

"Nah, I don't know him."

"What do you mean, 'Nah, I don't know him'? That's how you should talk to your father? I really don't like the way young people talk these days."

"Sorry . . ."

I knew that if this went on too long, Dad would blow a fuse, so I meekly apologized. I also wanted to talk to Worm while he was taking a break.

Resignedly, Dad said, "Go to bed soon."

"Um."

I went upstairs, put Teddy down, went into my room, and locked the door. I listened and heard Dad go into his bedroom. I lay down on my bed and took out my cell phone. Worm picked up after one ring.

"Hello. It's me."

Worm breathed a sigh of relief.

"Are you still at the convenience store?"

"No, I stood out too much. I'm lying in the parking lot out in back. I can see tons of stars."

"Are you tired?"

"Um," he said, sounding like a child.

"Text messaging's pretty convenient, isn't it?"

Worm had never had a cell phone up till now.

"Yeah, it sure is," he agreed, and stopped. "But this one's an old model and you can only send a hundred and twenty-eight letters at a time."

"Yeah, guess so."

Which is why the phone was cheap. I was a little annoyed, though Worm didn't seem to pick up on this.

"It's okay, you're the only one I'm gonna text."

"But you talked to Kirarin, too, didn't ya?"

"Who's that?"

"One of my pals. She's totally hot."

"Really," Worm said, not terribly interested.

"Going to Tachikawa and back in one day made me worn out. Good exercise, though."

I'd gone out to Tachikawa to meet up with Worm, then pedaled all the way over to Suginami to Toshi's, an incredible distance.

It was kind of a snide remark, but Worm didn't seem to care.

Instead, he asked, "Hey, tell me something. How come you talk like a guy? I thought it was weird when we talked on the phone yesterday. But when I met you today, you're kind of cute—although you dress like a guy. What's up with that?"

This was out of the blue, and I didn't know what to say. I never really thought about why. I went to a girls' school and was told I was kind of mannish, so as a kind of gag I started talking like a guy and then it became natural. Dahmer and Boku-chan also always used the rough word *ore* for "I," and I think it's the first-person pronoun that fits best. When I'm thinking about something or feeling something inside of me, I use the feminine word *atashi,* but someday I'm sure this will change to *ore,* too. Worm's pointed question made me remember that incident—the one when the transvestite grabbed my chest, yelled at me, and roughed me up. This curbed the secret feeling of closeness I was starting to have for him. So he's a guy, after all. The kind who hates women dressed as guys, who denounces them. Did that make him my enemy? I sullenly stayed quiet, but Worm went on.

"A while ago I saw the evening paper at the convenience store. An article about me. I wanted to see, like, what the world's thinking about it. It didn't seem real. It was like I was dreaming. I looked up and there on the TV was the front of my house and some reporter babbling away. 'What sort of ominous thing dwells in this suburban neighborhood? What happened to this boy who's disappeared? Is the same darkness in this boy hidden in this seemingly quiet neighborhood?' It felt so weird."

"D'ya feel like you wanna go back to the real world?"

"I can't," Worm said coolly. "This is my reality now."

"So why'd you make a reality like that happen? It's you who made things that way, right?"

I was a little irritated. I suffered more than anyone else because my mom died, and because I'm gay—but I wasn't responsible for these things. And now here was this guy who, just the day before, had created a new reality, one where he'd killed his mother.

"I don't know."

Worm didn't want to talk about it. Just like when I'd met him.

"I'd like you to pull yourself together and tell me about it."

"Why? Why do I have to tell somebody else? It's personal," he said.

"I want to know."

"How come?"

"I want to believe that if I'd been you, I'd have killed her, too."

Worm didn't say anything. Silence continued for a long time. I looked at the windowpane, the curtain still open. My blank face, cell phone pressed against it, was reflected in the glass. The glass was perfect, not a scratch on it.

The first time Worm called my cell phone was after dinner, when my dad and I were in the middle of a fight. Dad was so upset he could barely speak, all because I told him I wasn't going to take the college entrance exams.

"Then what do you plan to do with your life?"

How should I know? If I had to give a quick answer, all I could think of was working behind the counter of the Bettina, or else learning to be a transvestite. If I said that, my father would definitely cry. Dad's proud of working in the media, but he's actually a boring guy who's pretty conservative.

"So you're going to be like Winnie the Pooh, huh? Knock it off!" He was really pissed. "It might sound good right now, but what about later? Stop acting like a baby."

I wasn't acting like a baby. I really didn't have a clue what I should do. After I went into high school and my sexual orientation became clearer to me, I was faced with two choices: either deceive everybody, or come out of the closet. But I still hadn't decided which route to take, and so I had no energy to think about college. Those were the times when I was glad Mom wasn't alive anymore. I didn't say anything and Dad started in with one of his sermons. Grandma brought out some peaches she'd peeled and stealthily crept back to her room. I could sense that Dad was choosing his words carefully, aware that my grandparents were eavesdropping,

"If you don't go to college, you'll regret it. I've known a lot of young people who didn't go, so I know what I'm talking about. Once they go out into the world they finally realize how blessed they'd been and regret having thrown away the chance. The girl who's my assistant is like that. She told me she doesn't know why she didn't go to the photography department at the Japan Academy of Arts. She failed the exam once and never took it again. But I admire her. She got a job and is doing her best. She's found her own path in life, wanting to be a photographer. You don't even have that. You haven't gone out in the world. Once you do, you'll be sorry you didn't take this opportunity. But then it'll be too late."

It's not too late. I'm already out in what you call *the world*. A world of emotions that's different from what my old man's talking about. I wanted to tell him this, but that would mean revealing I was gay, and I wasn't ready for that. Irritated, all I could do was pretend to sulk.

"Anyway, you like the arts, so you should go somewhere where you can study that field."

"It's too late," I said, attempting a compromise. Saying it was too late was my way of buying time. I hated myself for it. Dad's face suddenly lit up.

"It's not too late! You can go to a cram school. I'll find out which one's good."

From the next room my grandpa cleared his throat in relief. It wasn't easy living there. After Mom died, even if Dad had wanted to move out and be free, he couldn't. He has a twenty-year mortgage and had built a house for two families to live in. Even if Grandpa and Grandma passed away, the land would most likely go to the immediate heir: me. If it came to that, I might kick Dad out, a thought that made me feel a whole lot better. Just then my cell phone rang from in the pocket of my shorts and my father pointed to it.

"Your cell phone's ringing."

The screen said the caller was Toshi.

"It's from Toshi."

Looking somewhat tired and unhappy, Dad reached for his cigarettes. He seemed relieved it wasn't a guy.

"Hey. What's up?"

"Sorry to bother you."

I was surprised to find it *was* a guy. Phone pressed to my ear, I slowly eased my way upstairs. Downstairs, my grandparents had come out and I could hear Dad explaining things to them. "Senior year in high school is a tough age," he was saying. "Hard to tell if they're adults or still kids."

"Who the heck are you?" I asked the guy on the phone. "And what're you doing with Toshi's phone?" I waited until I was safely back in my room.

"You're Kiyomi, aren't you?"

"Yeah, that's right."

Instinctively, I knew the guy had picked up Toshi's phone somewhere and was randomly dialing all the girls' names on it. My voice is so low hardly anyone ever guesses on the phone that I'm a girl.

Besides, the name Kiyomi could work for either guys or girls. The guy apologized weakly and was about to hang up.

"Hold on a sec, pal," I said. "I'm a girl. But how'd ya get hold of that phone?"

"I found it and thought I'd return it."

I told him all he had to do was dial the number under Home. "Got it," he said, and then said this: "Hey—if you're a girl how come you talk all rough like that?"

This pissed me off, so I asked him, "How the hell old are ya?"

"Seventeen. I'm a senior in high school."

"You're a real loser, you know that?"

I was just about to hang up when he said this:

"I, ah—killed my mother today."

I thought this was a great joke, so I played along.

"Yeah? I killed my mom three years ago."

This wasn't a lie. I might not have done it with my own hands, but inside it felt like I had.

They found out Mom had ovarian cancer just when I entered junior high in April. She passed away in October of my third year in junior high, so it was like my whole junior high school days were occupied by my mom's illness. Cancer takes a long time to kill you, so it's really rough on your family. It wasn't like she came to terms with it. There were some days when she did, I guess, seem calm about it, but other times she wailed about her fate like she was possessed by an evil spirit. She was only thirty-eight, and most of the time it was the latter. Dad was hardly ever at home—it made me think he might be having an affair—and Mom was so emotionally unstable that the rest of us didn't know how to handle her. One day she'd suddenly hug me tight and apologize, the next she'd push me away. We had to deal with these violent mood swings. I recoiled from this. I was worn out and had no idea how to handle it. On top of this was my dawning realization that I was a lesbian. I realized my mom was too preoccupied with her illness to think about my troubles, and I grew lonely, sad, and totally depressed. After agonizing over it for a while, I finally decided to abandon her. I decided in my heart that the moment she became sick was the moment she died. The person in the bed was a living corpse and nothing else.

When my mother was close to death, my father came to get me, but I refused to come out of my room.

"Come on. Your mother wants to see you."

"I'm not going," I said.

I held Teddy to me and kept on shaking my head.

"I know you're scared, but it's okay. She's dying and you should see her."

Dad was almost in tears, but I wasn't going to fall for that. Say I did go see her when she was dying and I had this phony smile like everything's all right, would that be it? What about *my* feelings? All kinds of outrageous thoughts ran through my mind.

"But Mom will be sad," Dad said.

"So what? Everybody's sad."

"Don't you feel sorry for her that she's dying? You're her only daughter."

Well, she's my only mother, too, I wanted to tell him. I didn't deserve this, either. I wasn't aiming to get revenge, just to get my mother, at least in her final days, to think about her relationship with me. My father gave up and left the room, and soon after this I heard this *ping* at the window. There was a crack in the glass. A small pebble must have hit it. Teddy was frightened and was shivering. I opened the window and looked outside. The sun had long since set and the streetlights were lit. The street was deserted. Not long after this the phone rang with the news that my mother had died.

"So what you mean is that pebble was your mother?" this guy on the phone said after hearing my story.

"I don't know. It sounds too much like a ghost story, so I never told anybody about it. You're the first."

"Why didn't you tell anybody?" he asked.

"I didn't want to. If I told them the truth, then—"

I stopped. Why in the world was I telling all this to some guy I'd never met?

"If you told the truth, then what? Tell me. I want to hear it."

He'd told me his secrets, so maybe I should tell him mine. I searched for the right words.

"I thought my mother was blaming me," I began. "That she hated me. When you hate someone like that, your spirit still hangs around and you can't properly pass on. That's when I started to get scared. Not scared of my mother or her ghost or anything. Scared of how strong the bonds between people can be. So when I decided I'd abandon my mother it felt like I'd murdered her."

"I know what you mean," the boy agreed. "It's the same with me."

"Did your mother really die?"

"I already told you," he yelled, irritated.

"Tell me how it happened."

"I'll tell you after I've got it all straight in my head. It's hard to explain—it was like it just—happened. But I do remember this one weird thing. When I grabbed my mother by the hair, I thought,

Wow, her hair's just like a woman's. I really felt like, Hey, she's a woman. But the person in front of me was just this crabby, complaining old bitch who was talking nonsense. It was like I thought, Shut the hell up! and pushed the off button on a machine."

A chill shot up my spine. His voice sounded like it was filtering up from some dark whirlpool. Even if he didn't kill her, I thought, I bet he beat up his mother.

He was ending our conversation. "The guy's making his rounds of the park."

"Where are you?"

"At Tachikawa Park."

"Can you stay overnight there?"

"If I hide I can," he said. "But the mosquitoes are terrible."

We agreed to meet the next day at the McDonald's in Tachikawa Station. He hesitated a little, but I pushed him to agree. I had to hear the rest of his story.

I knew beforehand from Toshi's phone call that what he said was true, but I'd felt right from the start that he was telling the truth. Otherwise, I never would have told him what I did.

When I actually met him the next day, he was sunburned, his red face all gloomy. He was skinny, too, like a string bean. His navy blue Nike T-shirt was kind of dirty, with bits of grass clinging to it. As he stood in the McDonald's trying to find me, other people looked at him funny. 'Cause he stank. They're gonna catch him any minute, I thought, and tried to think of how I could help him run far away.

"You're just what I expected," I told him. It was funny how Toshi's description of him fit perfectly.

"What'd Toshi say?"

"She said you're like a worm."

"That's awful!" He laughed. When he laughed, he was kind of cute.

"You smell bad," I said. "You gotta change your clothes."

"I've got only one change of clothes and don't want to waste them. It's so hot I thought I might as well just keep these on."

"Makes sense."

Worm didn't seem to hear me. He was staring vacantly out the window. The sun was going down, but the asphalt was still scorching.

"Is it true you're going to K High?"

Worm nodded, still gazing out the window.

"Aiming to get into Tokyo University?"

"I don't think I can anymore."

Don't think you can anymore? You better believe it. They're gonna run you through a ton of psychiatric tests, turn you into some guinea pig, then throw you into juvie. Society's erased you from its board, pal. You can forget about entrance exams and Tokyo University. What a moron! Still, I felt sympathetic toward this guy who just didn't get it.

"Have you got it all straight in your head now—about what happened?"

"Not yet," he said, looking out the window again. "I haven't really searched my conscience yet, so I guess I can't."

"Guess not."

Worm startled me by suddenly bolting straight up in his chair.

"I gotta go. I don't know why, but I feel like I've got to hurry."

"Where're ya going?"

"I don't know. Somewhere. I just feel like I have to go somewhere, *right now.*"

"Then you'd better go. Leave your bike, though. I gotta get it back to Toshi. You can take mine."

I motioned with my chin toward my bike parked outside. Worm looked kind of embarrassed.

"You rode it all the way here for me?"

I brought out a brand-new cell phone and laid it on the narrow little McDonald's table.

"You can have this, too," I said. "But give me back Toshi's."

Worm pulled out Toshi's phone from the pocket of his dirty jeans and tilted his head.

"Thanks. But why're you doing this?"

I had no idea. I was just waiting, and hoping, that he'd get his head together and let me in on something important, something I had to know.

"You better get going," I said.

Worm shoved the new cell phone, manual, and charger into his backpack and stood up. He turned his sulky narrow eyes to me. Birds of a feather, I thought, and waved to him. Worm clumsily made his way out of the place, bumping into the tiny tables as he left.

I sipped my iced coffee and gazed out the window. Worm went over to where my silver bike was, let out the side brake, sat down, then raised the seat. He sat down again and turned in my direction. His eyes were desperate. *I just feel like I have to go somewhere, right now.* "I understand totally. Just don't get caught," I muttered, then slurped down the rest of my coffee.

On TV once I saw this weird scene, a Japanese soldier getting pounded on the head with a hammer. He was getting completely worked over—besides the hammer, he was being stabbed with a sharpened stick and pummeled with flying kicks.

The people who were beating him up were an emaciated old Filipino man and woman, most likely taking revenge for what the Japanese had done to them during the war. Their positions reversed now, the old Filipino woman was whaling away at the soldier, putting everything she had into it like that was the only way she could get rid of the hatred inside her. The soldier had on a grubby T-shirt and a loincloth. Somehow he was still wearing his uniform cap. His hands were tied behind him and he stood there, staggering under the blazing sun. Whenever he was about to collapse, someone off-camera pulled on the rope that bound him, so he had to remain standing up straight.

My point is, at a moment like that, what is a person thinking? I was in elementary school when I saw this scene, and I found it incredible that the soldier looked so sleepy, like he was about to doze off. He had these vacant-looking eyes, half closed like he was going to fall asleep any minute, so you couldn't tell if he was feeling any pain. If it'd been me, I'd have been scared to death and would have cried and begged for it to end.

I remembered this scene because right now I'm so sleepy I can barely stand it. Abnormally sleepy. All the time I'm pedaling my bike I'm about to doze off. Maybe it's the weather, but it's weird I'd feel this way as I pedal down the blazing asphalt of the highway, inches from trucks whizzing by. It's not like I'm tired or anything.

All I've been doing since yesterday is tooling around on a girl's bike. It's been an easy trip so far. Whenever I see a convenience store I stop in to cool off, drink some water, read some manga. So there's no reason I should be so sleepy.

So maybe the situation I'm in now is like that of the Japanese soldier. Maybe I'm not aware of it, but my unconscious is trying to escape from reality. So I guess there's something to be afraid of.

Mother-killer. I never imagined I'd do something like that, but there it is. The shock of seeing that news program last night at the convenience store has started to make me jumpy. When I saw an article about it in the paper, I just thought, Hey, look at that! But TV is frightening.

What sort of ominous thing dwells in this suburban neighborhood? What happened to this boy who's disappeared? Is the same darkness in this boy hidden in this seemingly quiet neighborhood?

The newscaster's remarks were dumb, but when I saw this, it was the first time I realized what a mess I was in. Newspapers don't count, but once something hits TV it's all over. On news programs and talk shows people are endlessly analyzing this "darkness" in my heart. They'll all join forces and drone on and on about my mental state—commentators and newscasters, all with these know-it-all looks on their faces, gabbing away like they know what they're talking about. Isn't that slander? Even if they say something about me that's completely off the mark, though, I can't just laugh it off. 'Cause it's *me* they're talking about.

Just like with Sakakibara and those other murderers, I'll be in all the papers for days, and they'll gather experts together to endlessly debate changing the juvenile statutes. There'll be articles with my photo and the message I wrote in my grade school yearbook, some classmate will post my photo on the Internet, and all of it will be just more ammunition for the rumor mill. People who didn't like me will say whatever they like: "He was kind of gloomy, but never stood out in class, so I don't know much about him." "He always said hello, but I heard rumors that he tortured cats in the neighborhood."

When I think of being on the run all over Japan with everybody in the country trying to track me down, it feels like my fate is to keep on running forever. Not like there's anyplace for me to run to. Like in Stephen King's *The Running Man*, taxi drivers and convenience store clerks are going to phone the cops, telling them that that guy on TV was just here.

Speaking of Stephen King, I really like him. *The Running Man* and *Carrie*. I read *The Long Walk* twice. *Battle Royale* isn't by King, but I read that twice, too. Most of the kids I know read only manga, but I prefer novels. Novels are closer to real life than manga, it's like they show you the real world with one layer peeled away, a reality you can't see otherwise. They're deep, is what I'm saying. Which makes me sort of a weirdo in my class. The guys in my class see only the outer surface. Same with their parents. Guess they find that makes living easier, like that's the smart way to approach life. What a bunch of assholes.

I have to keep doing something, I'm so sleepy. Half awake, I focus on the scenery passing by. Boring scenery along a main road. A pachinko place, a karaoke place, a used-car lot. A ramen shop, a family restaurant. All of them with their windows shut tight and the AC going full blast. A tin roof of a garage reflects the bright sun, hot as a frying pan.

But it's like none of this is part of my world anymore. Ordinary scenery has transformed. Or I should say it's *me* that's changed. If I go into a pachinko place or a karaoke place, I know I won't feel the way I used to about them. I'll never feel the way I used to—

ever again. Do you know what I mean? If somebody had told me all this before, I would have said, What the hell are you talking about? But there's this gap now between my world and other people's. And I'm totally alone.

People are part of the scenery, too. The truck driver talking on his CB as he passes me, the middle-aged guy stifling a yawn as he drives a white delivery van. The woman with a small child on the seat beside her, the elementary school pupil crossing the road. It's like all these men and women—everybody—are in a different world from me. In *their* world, time just stretches on endlessly, today the same as yesterday, tomorrow the same as today, the future the same as tomorrow.

I feel like I'm racing alone through a desert on some distant planet, like Mars. Everything's changed from two days ago. Everything's divided now into *before* then and *after* then—*then* meaning the day I killed my mother. My actions created a turning point, a crossroads, in my own life. And now I finally understand the fear that Japanese soldier felt. People who experience this kind of a crossroads are afraid. And so sleepy they can't stand it.

As these thoughts kept a lazy pace with my pedaling, I got so sleepy I really couldn't stand it anymore. I wondered if I should stop my bike by the side of the road and take a nap. I looked around for a good place to sleep, but there wasn't any, just cheap-looking houses and shops, not what I wanted—a bench or a small patch of grass. God, I'm so sleepy! *So sleepy.* I want to crawl into my own bed and sleep forever.

My room is a corner room on the southeast side of the house. An eight-mat room with wooden flooring, French bed, double mattress. Plus my own TV. It's the biggest, best room in the house—not that I chose it myself or anything. Two years ago, when we moved in, when that trouble happened, Mom announced we were leaving the apartment building and moving here to a single-family home.

After we moved she said, "We'll make Ryo's room the sunniest one on the second floor." She always says these "nice" things, taking care of her precious son.

Since that was already decided, my old man said he'd use the Japanese-style room on the second floor as his study. A study? Don't make me laugh. All he's got are dusty old sets of collected works. Those aren't books—they're *furniture*. And how about all those records he's collected since college? He never listens to them. *Hello!* Ever heard of CDs? We got MP3s and DVDs, too, in case you didn't know. And don't give me all that crap about how great analog sounds, okay? You don't know anything, yet all you do is brag, you clown. Where'd you learn all that useless stuff? From some bar hostess? Women aren't falling all over doctors anymore. Okay, so you bought a computer, but do you ever use it? You're just trying to look cool. Do you know that I sneak into your room, surf the Web, and play around on porn sites? As long as you don't, there's nothing you can do about it. Stop showing off, you jerk. Why can't you see that I think you're a total loser? You always brag about being a doctor, but you just work in a nothing little clinic. No better than some office worker. If you don't like it, why don't you become the head of a huge hospital and use your money to get me into Harvard? 'Cause you *can't,* that's why.

Mom doesn't have her own room. She uses the parlor, but that's different, that's public space. Does this mean we have a public park in our house? A public restroom? I don't need my own room, she said, because I have the "utility room." Give me a break. "Utility"— what the hell's that mean? "Identity" I know, but "utility"? What? You're telling me to look it up in a dictionary? No way. I only want to use an electronic dictionary. And it has to be one that's an unabridged dictionary and also has an encyclopedia. Don't you get it? I'm telling you to buy me one!

When I said that, she ran right out and bought one for me. I was sick and tired of being with her. If you'll give me anything, how about giving me your life? I wanted to say. I didn't exactly ask to be your son, so give me your life. Did she know how much I despised her? The thought that I had to be with this old hag for the rest of my days depressed me, like my life was already over. You know what that feels like? *Total depression.*

I feel relieved that my old lady's no longer here, even though I'm the one who killed her. I still get angry when I think of her and it makes it hard to get sleepy. So thinking of her maybe is a good way to combat this sleepiness that's come over me.

My mother was a total idiot. I don't know when it was I realized this. Probably the year after I started cram school, around fifth grade. Every day she gave me a stupid sermon.

The most outstanding people in the world, she'd lecture me, aren't just intelligent, but the ones who make an effort. It's easy to substitute other words into this formula. Let's try it—it's fun. Not just intelligent, but those who make an effort. Not just stylish, but those who make an effort. Not just athletic, but those who make an effort. Not just those from a good family, but those who make an effort. Not just the rich, but people who make an effort. Not just the lucky, but people who make an effort. In other words, you first have to have the one good quality, and only then can you be considered outstanding.

Which raises the question of whether Mom herself is an outstanding person. When I was in fifth grade, I started to have my doubts whether she'd cleared any of the hurdles on the road to becoming outstanding. Let's face it, she wasn't especially smart or pretty. She had absolutely no sense of style. Zero athletic ability. And making an effort? Forget about it. So where did she get off lecturing me? Finally, though, I realized something. Mom was convinced she was an outstanding person. She was convinced she was smart, pretty, from a good family. And besides, she was married to a doctor, with a smart son, and worked hard every day. I was just a kid, but I was shocked all the same. She's not playing with a full deck, this old lady. *Unbelievable.*

"Fortunately, Ryo, you're smart, so I want you to make more of an effort. It's important to do your best."

I don't know how many times I heard this. Somewhere along the line, though, it hit me: I'm really not all that smart. This was soon after I got into K Junior High, which is considered one of the hardest private junior highs to get into. The first exam we had there, of the two hundred and fifty kids in my grade level, I wasn't even in the top two hundred. That's weird, I thought. But the next test turned out the same. And the one after that. The whole five years I've been in junior high and high school it's been more of the same.

Mom panicked. I did, too, but she panicked first. You know why, right? 'Cause this smashed to bits the theory she kept pounding into my head. If I put this much effort into it and was never rewarded, then the premise of her theory had to be wrong. I wasn't as smart as my mom and I had thought. If Mom had only realized how stupid she was herself, she would have understood much earlier that I wasn't the sharpest crayon in the box.

Which is why she blames me, because I'm dumb. One time she stared intently at me, those eyes behind her glasses, sizing me up like she'd never seen me before. Finally she managed this: "Ryo, are you popular with girls?" Are you serious? Since I entered an all-boys school, I haven't spoken to any girls. Haven't gotten a phone call from any girl, or a letter. I'm my old man and old lady's kid, after all. The offspring of a hick and a hag. And wasn't it my old lady who dumped me in a place where there aren't any girls? Yet here she is asking if I'm a chick magnet.

She was asking this because she realized her education policy was a failure. She understood that I'm not very smart, not good-looking, and that maybe I won't have such a happy life after all. What a dolt. Take a look in the mirror, I wanted to tell her. How about considering your own crummy life before you rag on me?

All these memories were getting me angry and upset, and completely got rid of my sleepiness. I saw a convenience store off to my left. Convenience stores are my stations. Can't live without them. I happily stopped my bike and went inside.

After the blazing inferno outside, the cold air felt better than good—it totally revived me. The store was still new and was spacious. There was one middle-aged woman behind the register wearing a visor and a smock that didn't suit her. She was glaring at the customers who were standing at the magazine rack leafing through the magazines. An old guy, probably the manager, was bent over some shelves, doing his best to straighten up the bento section. They didn't look like they were used to the work. A convenience store veteran would never be so angry at people standing around reading magazines and manga for free.

In convenience stores, the entrance is the coolest spot, since they keep the AC at full blast there, shooting out dry, cold air to keep away the heat from outside. So I stood there at the entrance for a while, cooling off my overheated body. The cold air crystallized my sweat. I had the illusion that my whole skin was covered with a thin layer of glittering white salt. With my salt suit on, I was

better than any other person around. I am a mother-killer, after all!
And I'm on the run! Only a tiny percentage of mankind could do
what I did. I can get away with *anything*.

I grabbed a 1.5-liter bottle of water from the fridge and took it
over to the register. Paid for it and impatiently drank it down. I was
so parched I couldn't stop. I gulped down over half before I put
the cap back on. Then I turned to the woman behind the register,
who was staring at me with a troubled look, hand over her nose.

"Could I use your restroom, please?" I asked.

The woman turned around to the middle-aged guy. He tossed
the bentos aside and trotted over.

"I'm sorry, sir," he said. "We don't have a restroom."

"What's that then?"

I know where the restrooms are in convenience stores, almost
always next to the refrigerator. I pointed to a likely door.

"That's a storage room."

The man was holding his nose, too. Two out of three convenience stores turn me down when I ask to use the bathroom, so I
wasn't overly disappointed. Five other places in a row had said no,
so all I thought was that the percentage was going down. The old
guy, though, had to go and add this:

"I'm sorry, sir, but since it bothers other customers I'd appreciate it if you'd drink outside. And please use the restroom somewhere else. My apologies."

I'm bothering other people? What did he mean? Was it my salt
suit? I sniffed my T-shirt, and it did smell kind of gross—a kind of
sour, weird smell. It had been two days since I left home. I hadn't
washed the shirt or taken a bath—was that all it took to get like
this? I swam in a pool, but I guess that didn't work. The blazing
sun had turned me into this smelly guy people wanted to avoid.
Just being at home meant I wouldn't get smelly—the thought

impressed me, somehow, in a weird sort of way. I'd washed my face and hands at a park, but couldn't wash my T-shirt or jeans. I scratched my head.

"You're telling me to get out?"

"No, it's that we'd rather you didn't drink here or use the bathroom. So if you don't mind . . ."

So he was using the restroom as a pretext for getting me out of there. I ignored the old guy and, water bottle in hand, sauntered over to the magazine and book rack. When I got there a fat guy engrossed in a porno magazine gave me a strange look and tossed it aside. Two high school girls also grimaced and edged away. I blithely opened up the latest copy of *JUMP* and started leafing through it. The fat guy left the store, so I opened up the porno mag he'd been reading. It was full of pretty girls with their legs spread. I wanted the magazine but didn't want to spend the money on it, so I stared hard at the photos, to burn the images into my brain. "He stinks," some girl's voice whispered from the next aisle over. The high school girls. In times like these I always want to say this: "Hey, I go to K High, just so you know!" I'm such an idiot. But the thought also hits me that the guys at K High who really *are* smart would never brag like that. They're much too clever.

So in the final analysis the only use for the education my old lady so highly prizes is to brag about it in front of others. Nobody outside K High knows I'm at the bottom of the class, or that the teachers make fun of me. The whole thing's crappy. But I had to stay there, stay put. Junior and senior high—six years! "You'll be studying for college entrance exams soon," my old lady always told me, "so you just have to hang in there a little longer." Hang in there for *what*? She didn't understand me at all. I'd run out of patience a long time ago.

I noticed something and turned around. The manager was

standing there, timidly trying to figure out whether he should say something. Remembering I was on the run, I decided to get out. No good for me to stand out too much. My cell phone rang just when I got outside. It was from Yuzan, the girl who helped me.

"Hello. It's me."

I probably shouldn't say this, but talking to her is just like talking to a guy. Doesn't do a thing for me. Girls should have a higher, cuter voice. Why? 'Cause they're a different life-form, that's why. So when I talk to this Yuzan I always feel like complaining. But I guess that makes me just as bad as my old lady—always wanting things to go my way. Guess we share the same blood after all. I smiled bitterly.

"Hold on a sec," I said.

I looked for a shady place, but there wasn't any in front of the convenience store. Just the roar of trucks and the blazing sun. I was bowled over by the heat reflecting off the concrete. My salt suit was melting, dripping down my skin, and sticking to it. I found a truck parked in the parking lot and slumped down in its shade.

"What d'ya want?" I asked.

"Are you doing okay?"

"Yeah. I wound up sleeping in a convenience store parking lot last night. Too many mosquitoes when you sleep outdoors. Then I ate some rice balls from the store and have been riding since morning."

"Where're you at now?"

"I don't know. Out in the sticks," I said, glancing around me. Somewhere out in Saitama Prefecture. "Around Kumagaya, I think."

"Supposed to be a really hot place. You okay?"

Yuzan spoke very fast. The heat must have been messing up my brain, 'cause I couldn't talk right.

"I'm okay. But what's happening with the cops?"

"Toshi says they're coming by every day. But what'd you expect? I saw your old man a little while ago. They had your mom's funeral this morning. It was terrible, your old man was bawling."

He broke down? It felt like it had nothing to do with me. Killing my mom, wanting to kill my dad later, too—under this blazing sun it all felt unreal, like a myth from some far-off land. Were these people really my parents? I'd been thinking about this before, while pedaling my bike—the whole *before then, after then* thing. As I mulled over my hatred of my mom, it felt like I'd left *after then* way behind—and had crossed over to a completely different world. What the hell's going to happen to me? With this salt suit on, am I no longer going to be human? For the first time, I started to feel worried.

"I wonder what's going to happen to me."

"Whatever happens, happens," Yuzan said coolly. That part of her, I don't like, I thought. I don't know what her story is, but it's like whenever I try to get a little closer she gets all cold and stand-offish. Still, she's curious about me. But I can't figure her out, and I don't like people I can't figure out.

"Did anybody from my school come to the funeral?" I asked.

"No idea. I don't think there were any high school students there."

"To them I was just a piece of trash they never noticed."

Yuzan chuckled. "Cooler to be a piece of trash."

Her words rescued me, and I felt strong all of a sudden.

"So being on the run is cool?" I asked.

"Yeah. What I mean is—what are you going to do now?"

Her voice was filled with sympathy and curiosity. It was like she wanted me to be her stand-in in some great adventure.

"I just have to keep running."

"Where?" she asked.

"I have no clue."

I really didn't. Yuzan gave this big sigh, like a little kid.

"I wanna go with you somewhere."

"There's nowhere I can go."

This time it was my turn to be abrupt. Yuzan had helped me, but it didn't feel like I was dealing with a girl. Besides, she was a complicated type, kind of unapproachable. A gloomy person who blamed herself 'cause she was convinced her mother's illness and death were her fault. As I talked with her on the phone I was thinking, You and I are very different. I'm much colder.

"Guess you're right," she said. "Hey, is it okay if I tell my friends your cell number? They all want to call you."

"No problem," I said.

I don't know why, but this idea got me excited. When I stole that girl Toshi's bike and cell phone, what was most fun was being able to talk with all the girls whose numbers were in the contacts list. I'd like to meet the one named Kirarin.

Yuzan acted all cool, like she'd seen right through me. "I see— so you're a regular guy after all. Okay, I'll let 'em know."

Damn, I thought, and was silent. If Yuzan tips off the cops I'm in a world of trouble. I hung up and took another swig of water. I was hungry but didn't feel like going back to the convenience store. I plopped down next to one of the truck's wheels. God, some *yakiniku* would taste great right about now.

"Hey, get outta the way."

This voice came from above me and when I opened my eyes, there was a young man standing there. Blond hair and sunglasses, running shoes and shorts. The driver of the truck. A tough-looking guy.

"Sorry."

As I stood up the guy grimaced.

"I think I'm gonna puke, you stink so much."

"Sorry," I said again. It pissed me off that I had to apologize to some guy I didn't even know. I went over to the bike rack. I checked out an old lady's bike, a black one, saw it was unlocked, and hopped aboard. Yuzan's silver bike was cool-looking but stood out too much. Plus, it felt good to dump that pushy girl's bike.

The old lady's bike was heavy. I pedaled off on the main road again and thought that I'd better go over the day my world changed or else I'd get sleepy again. Just then the cell phone rang. I stopped the bike by the side of the road and answered it. First, though, I hid the bike in some bushes so nobody would spot it and crouched down there.

"It's me. Toshi. From next door."

Yuzan didn't waste any time giving her my number.

"Oh, hey. Yuzan told me they had my old lady's funeral today."

"That's right," Toshi said, her voice kind of gloomy. "I'm calling from my cram school right now, but your father and relatives were all crying at the funeral. My parents, too, and I couldn't help crying, either. Hey, I can understand your wanting to run away, but don't cause any trouble for Yuzan, okay? That'd make her an accomplice."

Who the hell does this girl think she is? Sounds exactly like my old lady. I was really disappointed. I mean, it's like I murdered my mother for *her* sake. That's why, right after I did it, when I ran across her outside it made me really happy. I offed my old lady for you, I wanted to laugh and say to her, so what're you gonna do for *me* now? It was all for you, I wanted to tell her. But all I could get out was "Sure is hot today." Pathetic.

"I'm sorry, but it's really hot here, so could you call back later?"

"That's pretty rude. And after I went to the trouble of calling you. See you."

She hung up the phone. For a moment, I was afraid she'd rat on me, tell 'em what happened that day, but then I figured that by now everybody knew I'd whacked my old lady, so who cares. I sat there in the bushes, hugging my knees. It was strange, I thought, why all these weird girls like Yuzan and Toshi were interested in me. Was I their hero? That was enough to cheer me up.

A *matricidal murderer.* I knew I'd done something really huge, but thinking of it in those terms made me feel kind of strange. And the more I ran, the stranger it felt. I lay down on the grass and gazed up at the sky. While I was lying there, I wondered, What was Toshi up to at that cram school of hers? As I imagined her, I got an erection.

From the east side veranda of my room I can just barely see into Toshi's room. Her desk is near the window and when I'm lucky I can catch a glimpse of her studying there through a gap in the lace curtains. When that happens, I turn off all the lights in my room and peek out. I can see her face in profile, lit by the lamp beside her. Sometimes, probably when she's reading manga, she laughs out loud or else she frowns. You're not so bright, I want to tell her, so why bother with studying? What's the point? You're a girl, so that's plenty! That's enough to see you through life, right? Who cares if you don't do well in school? That's what went through my head. I had a lot of mixed feelings toward girls for a long time. And why not? Girls don't have to compete—just being a girl means guys will fall all over themselves for you.

Ever since I realized I'm not too bright, I couldn't help but think that maybe girls are way smarter than me. And thinking about Toshi in particular gave me an inferiority complex, 'cause she wasn't so bad-looking, and probably a whole lot happier than me. I can't explain it, but I started to feel that way. Whenever I ran across her at the station, she'd nod a hello, but for some reason I couldn't nod back. I know you might think that's no big deal, but I started to feel inferior to her. A cleverer guy would be able to get to know her better, but every time I thought of talking to her she'd give me this indifferent look and then vanish.

I always heard people laughing in her house, like they were having fun. Whenever that happened I'd think that homes with young girls are the cheerful ones, and that'd make my complex even worse. I might go to a school like K High, but that means absolutely nothing to anybody else. Still, my old lady, the moron, is convinced it's a big deal. The upshot is I'm crushed between the world's opinion and the old lady's. It's like that's the duty I have to perform.

Soon after we moved into our house I discovered that from the veranda of my old man's study you can see into the bathroom in Toshi's house. If the window is open you can see the bathtub. The time I first realized this, unfortunately it was her father who was in the bath. Her mother was always more cautious and made sure to shut the window tightly. Toshi, though, was a little slow on the uptake, and sometimes she'd take a bath without closing the window, especially if her father bathed first and left it open.

Once I found out all this, I started to look forward to watching her when she was studying, and whenever she went to take a bath I'd crouch down on the veranda, waiting. There was only a one-in-twenty chance of success. And it only worked in the summer, when the window was open, when her father had taken a bath before her. Even when everything fell into place, if my old man was in his study, forget about it.

On that particular day it must have been divine intervention, because everything went perfectly. Toshi turned out the light next to her desk and seemed to be heading off to the bath. I quickly went over to the window, stuck my face out, and peeked down at the bathroom. Steam was coming out, so I knew the window was open. Her father must have just taken his bath. Fantastic! Totally excited, I went out of the room and halfway down the stairs to check out what was going on below. Dad had come home already but I could hear him still eating dinner.

I slipped off quietly to his study and sneaked out to the veranda. Down below, Toshi was yelling something. Probably she was pissed 'cause her dad had left the bath a mess. I could hear water splashing. I sat there, waiting in anticipation, concerned a little about what my old man was doing. And the moment I'd been waiting for finally came. Toshi, naked, stepped into the tub, her legs momentarily spread wide. *Yes!* I did a quick fist pump, and at that exact moment somebody grabbed me by the hair from behind.

"What do you think you're doing?"

It was my mom, keeping her voice down. Both hands clutching my hair, she dragged me back into the old man's study, trying not to make any noise. And then back into my own room.

"Nothing special," I said.

"You were peeking into their house! That's disgusting. You're scum, you know. Human scum."

The old lady had taken off her makeup and was in her pj's, light blue pj's she'd bought at Peacock. Without her penciled eyebrows she looked homely and weird, plus her stomach was sticking out. You're the one who's disgusting scum, I wanted to tell her, and besides, why do I have to be yelled at by somebody like you?

"Sorry that I'm scum."

"You should be. This is all you do instead of studying. What in the world are you thinking? What about college entrance exams? You're a criminal, you know that? Why are you doing this?"

"A criminal?"

"That's right," she said. "A peeping Tom. You did the same thing in our old place and that's why we had to move. We had to get out of there before people found out about you, and it was very hard for Father and me."

"You just moved because you wanted to build a single-family home."

The old lady's face stiffened.

"How can you say that? People were about to find out about what you were up to, so we had to take off. Father and I were worried sick because we didn't want anything to hurt your future. It wasn't because of me. Something's *wrong* with you. What should we do? What could you possibly be thinking? What should we do?"

What should we do? What should we do? What should we do? The old lady glared at me, demanding a reply. Behind her silver-framed glasses, her eyes were bulged and burned with anger and contempt. It shocked me to think that a moron like this had contempt for me. Her anger was really jealousy, I suddenly realized. I mean, she was so totally angry. Shut up, old bag! *Maybe I should just kill her.* The thought sprang up in my mind. If she was out of the way, imagine how free I'd be. As long as she's around I'll never be free. She'll decide which university I should go to, pick out who I should marry, and wind up bossing my kids around. You can count on it.

"I'm going to tell Father what happened here," she said, and left the room. Not that the old man could say anything. He doesn't scare me. I'm taller than him, and stronger. Predictably, after a while the old man lumbered upstairs and without a word shut himself in his study. Tomorrow, I decided, after the old man's gone to work, I'm going to murder my old lady. With the metal bat in the corner of my room. Then I'll really be a criminal. Excellent. The Triple Crown: a criminal, a pervert, and a mother-killer. Imagining the bat humming down on the old lady's head, I took a couple of practice swings. But what she'd just said was still floating around in my mind.

People were about to find out what you were up to, so we had to take off.

Here's what happened. Before we came to Suginami-ku, until I was a freshman in high school, we lived in a suburban town with a population of about 150,000. In this huge housing project with about two hundred other families. The kind of huge apartment building you see everywhere, with long open hallways and tricycles and co-op boxes outside every door.

But that's where I was brought up, so I liked that town and our building. There were still fields around our apartment, and my friends and I played baseball there until it got dark. On rainy days we'd chase each other around the building. Most of my friends lived in the building, so we were all pretty much from the same sort of background.

Mom, though, hated the apartment. She said it was constructed shabbily, that you could hear people talking through the walls and sounds from above and below. Her real complaint, though, was that this apartment didn't measure up to her idea of the good life. Which to her meant a single-family home within the Tokyo city limits. You're a doctor, she told Dad, but look at us, living in the same sort of place as people who just work down the street. Dad just gave a contented laugh. What a stupid couple. After I passed the exam to get into K High, the old lady complained about this more and more. "I hate this place, I hate it!" she said.

Since I was happy living there, I didn't want her to get her way. Plus, a young couple moved in next door, which suddenly made me oppose moving even more. Because every single night I could hear them groaning and sighing.

My room and their bedroom were right next door to each other. In most of the apartments, the six-mat room was the children's room and the Japanese-style room, the same size next to it, was the parents' bedroom. Which meant that in your typical three-bedroom apartment the kids' room was separated from the neighbor adults' bedroom by just a wall. Talk about racy. As soon as I heard them start to groan I'd clap my ear to the wall. The young woman next door was very friendly, with a cute face like a charming little kitten. Her hair hung down straight, like a junior high girl's, exactly the way I like it. To imagine that young woman giving off groans like that!

Hearing them wasn't enough. I wanted to see them in the act. So I quietly opened the door to the veranda and leaned out. There was only a plywood partition separating our veranda from theirs, a board that was flimsy, so in case of a fire it could be easily broken through. All I had to do was get around that and I could spy into the couple's bedroom where they were going at it. Damn, I thought, what I'd give to be the Invisible Man.

Pretty soon I was getting all hot and bothered not just by the nighttime goings-on but thinking about what the woman next door was doing during the day, when her husband was gone and she was alone. Maybe she was getting off by herself? I'd love to see that, I thought. One day I skipped out on school and while Mom was out shopping I went out on the veranda and peeked around the partition. The curtains were closed, though, and I couldn't see anything. I was disappointed, but just then I noticed that she'd hung out her laundry to dry. Her tiny panties were all hanging from a round little dryer hanger. They were so pretty I reached out to try to touch them. I couldn't quite reach them, so I went back inside and brought out a dust mop. But I still couldn't get them. My arms got tired, and just when I was taking a break, a piece of thread wafted down from above. I looked up and two floors above us a lady was airing out her futons. She was a friend of my old lady's, I'm sure, someone she got to know through the co-op. Unconcerned, the woman went on beating her futon. Damn. I went back inside.

That night my old lady came up to me with this scary look on her face.

"What in the world were you up to during the day? Tell me."

"Nothing," I said.

"You were trying to get something from next door, weren't you?"

"No, I wasn't. I dropped an exam answer sheet and was just trying to pick it up."

My mom thought about this for a minute. I thought I'd conned her, but she shook her head.

"You should have just knocked on their door. I'll do that right now."

"No way!" I yelled, but off she went. I waited thirty minutes, then an hour, and she didn't come back. I was getting worried. Finally she came back, her eyes all red and puffy from crying.

"We can't live here anymore," she said.

What was going on? I didn't do anything *that* bad. I stayed silent, while Mom made a big show of crying.

"Maybe I've been a bad mother. I can't believe you'd do something like this."

"What did they say?"

"The husband answered the door and said there wasn't any

exam paper around. He said that he didn't have any proof, but it looked like you were trying to steal his wife's panties. He said one pair was lying on the ground and it looked suspicious. What if your school found out about this? What then? The husband said they wouldn't make a big deal out of it or anything because of your age, but I can't stand living here anymore!

"I can't believe it, can't believe it, we can't stay here anymore," she kept repeating, crying hysterically. The upshot was we left there soon after and moved here. In the beginning, after we moved, Mom seemed to have forgotten all that had happened and was happy. The nearby supermarket made her ecstatic: "They have my favorite salad dressing there!" she'd say. "And can you believe it—they carry pie sheets! It's a much higher class of customers here." When she found out that Toshi lived next door, though, she gradually grew more cautious.

"You can't see her room from yours, can you, Ryo?" she asked. How stupid can you get, I thought. *You're* the one who decided this would be my room! I didn't bother answering. And then there was this whole new incident with Toshi in the bath. You understand how disgusted I was with my mom? She was constantly smothering me. When I was in the bath myself, for instance, she'd be hovering outside next to the sink and I couldn't even come out when I finished. God, I hate her!

On the fateful day, I slept until eleven, with the AC on full blast. Just about the time when my old lady would come and try to get me up. But I was ready for her. The desire to kill her hadn't wavered since the day before. I got out of bed and grabbed my aluminum bat. I had on an old T-shirt instead of pajamas, in case there was a lot of blood. And a pair of boxers. I thought about doing it naked, but that would look stupid. I heard someone coming upstairs, noisier than usual. The old lady must be pissed about something again. Excellent. She knocked on my door and opened it.

"Are you going to sleep all day?" she complained.

She stopped, surprised at how chilly my room was. As I raised the bat I shouted out and she looked up at my hands. She shouted, too—"Stop it!" she yelled.

I swung the bat down and she leaped back out the door. *Strike one.* The bat slammed against the top of my bookshelf, banging off the pile of manga on top and shattering the lightbulb in the lamp next to my desk. The old lady scrambled down the stairs. Hey— you're not bad, I thought. She was pretty damn fast. I slowly came out of my room and came down after her. When she saw that I still had the bat in my hands, she dropped the phone she was holding. I placed it neatly back where it belonged and grabbed her hair. She struggled and finally broke free. I slammed the bat against the back of her head. It made a solid crunch but wasn't a direct hit. *Foul ball.* Blood dripping down her head, she staggered over to the bathroom. Probably thought she could lock herself inside. I raced after her and whacked her again on the back of her head. Smush! Sounded good, but it was still a bit off center. Another foul ball. Blood splattered out on my face. The old lady fell forward, head over heels, and collapsed, shattering the glass door to the bath-room. She was still alive. Her hair was matted with blood as she crawled toward the kitchen.

"You'll . . . be a criminal . . ." she moaned.

"I know. And I don't give a shit."

She nodded, but I could see the blood drain out of her face. It looked like she was dead. So the last one wasn't a foul ball after all, but a clean hit. Finally, the woman who gave birth to me, raised me, ordered me around, yelled at me, turned me into a sex maniac, who complained all the time, was dead. And I'm the one who killed her. I suddenly felt light and airy, like a balloon. Puffy. Swollen. I tossed the bat aside and sank down, exhausted, to the floor.

From the grass I could hear the low electric buzzing of some insects. Something must be up with my brain, I thought. Maybe something's seriously wrong with me. I don't feel even a bit of guilt. Holding my head, I stood up. The handles of the bike must be burning hot 'cause of the sun. This random thought was cruising through my head when the cell phone rang. It had to be Toshi.

"Yeah?"

"Hi, my name's Kirari Higashiyama. We talked before."

She had a high, clear voice. Different from Toshi's calm voice, or Yuzan's attempts to talk like a guy. Or that girl Terauchi with her gloomy voice. It made me happy.

"Yeah, I remember."

"Yuzan told me the number. So what are you doing now?"

"Just thinking, I guess. Or daydreaming. About all kinds of things."

"Really? Hey, are the police after you, or can we talk for a while?"

She sounded sympathetic. This girl didn't seem like she'd be much of a bother. An image came to me of the woman who lived next door in our old apartment building. If this girl was like her, that'd be cool.

"I don't know. Hey, babe, how 'bout we—?"

"Everybody calls me Kirarin."

Kirarin. I was too embarrassed to call her that silly name.

"Could we meet?" I asked.

"Are you sure?"

She hesitated, but I could tell she was curious. Maybe I really had become these girls' hero. Happy and excited, I wiped the sweat off my forehead.

C ould we meet?"
Worm sounded just like the guys I meet through text messaging when they phone me. Kind of fawning and brazen, like they know exactly what I want. Like all they're thinking about is getting it on.

"Are you sure?" I asked him hesitantly, but I was disappointed as usual. Hmm . . . so even a pumped-up young mother-killer like Worm wants to hit on girls. I'd been hoping he'd have a bit more backbone than that. Yet unconsciously my fingers started moving like I was typing out a text message. *Sure, I want to meet you, too. I'm all by myself today and kind of lonely.* A total lie.

I've only recently started playing around on chat-room sites. I'd type in a message like, *I'm hoping to hook up with someone right away. I'm sixteen, and going to a private high school.* In a flash I'd get nearly a hundred replies. From guys who are pretty sure this wasn't really a high school girl, but who are still dying to hook up. Idiotic.

I'd like to meet you. I'm eighteen, six-foot-one, and am into karate—sometimes you get those types. And then I type back: *You're really tall. That's cool. I'm only four-ten. Do you like small girls?* It's a game of mutual lies flying back and forth. I wondered if Worm wanted to play this game with me. If he does, I thought, he's a total idiot. I decided I'd tease him a bit.

"Where can I meet you?"

Worm hesitated. "It's not like I don't trust you or anything, but you won't tell the cops, will you?"

"Sounds like you don't trust me."

I said this in an intentionally high, weak voice like he really had hurt me. I've gotten pretty good at using my voice like this. It's a phone call, after all, so you can't see the other person's face. Guys are all suckers for a sweet, high-pitched voice. And Worm was typical. He started to get a bit flustered.

"No, I trust you," he said. "It's just that I have to be careful. They're after me."

They're after me—he sounded almost proud. You don't have any guts at all, I wanted to tell him. You killed your own mother, didn't you? What do you expect? Of *course* they're going to be after you. You're a criminal!

"Well—okay, then."

In situations like this I always act a little disappointed but keep it short and sweet. I don't pursue it any further because girls have guys after them all the time, so I know how it feels to be pursued. If you play too easy to get, you'll regret it. The kind of guys I'm attracted to are the ones who don't dig too far either.

"Kumagaya. Do you know it?"

"How come you went that far away?"

"It's superhot." Worm sighed. "I'd like to lug around an air conditioner with me."

Well, you're the one who ran away, I felt like saying. I started to feel a little cold and cruel. Give me a break—you murdered your own mom. So don't complain about a little heat!

"Come to the station," he said. "I'm on a bike, so I can't go too far in this heat."

Well, Worm, you've got a bit of an ego, don't you think? Asking a girl you're meeting for the first time to go all the way out to Kumagaya? Can't be many guys who'd do that. I gave him one of my patented lies.

"I'll come over right now. I'll call you when I get to the station."

"Cool. I'll be waiting."

Go all the way to Kumagaya when it's ninety-five degrees out? Not in this heat. Still, you don't get many opportunities to talk with a mother-murderer. This might be my only chance. Plus, Worm doesn't seem to like Toshi or Yuzan that much. I guess I should consider this a kind of honor, if I'm the only one he's asked to meet. I suddenly got all excited at the chance, and decided I'd better ask Teru for advice before I did anything.

Teru's a good friend of mine. A different kind of friend from Toshi, Terauchi, or Yuzan. We always have a lot to talk about, so it's fun to be with him. So much fun I've even thought we should do a make-believe marriage. Teru's gay. He's twenty-one and a freelancer. Until a while ago he drove a delivery truck, but then he landed a job creating Web sites. I knew he was in the middle of work, but I went ahead and called anyway.

"Hey, Teru, what's up?"

"I'm making a home page for this artist who makes these strange dyed fabrics. Soybean-flour and squid-ink colored fabrics. I saw some of the actual works and they were a really sickening color."

"But you're lucky you have work," I said.

"You're on summer vacation, right? You're the lucky one."

I loved Teru's sort of helpless, slow yet gentle way of talking. I first met him one day when I was wandering around Shibuya. He's the one who stopped me, and I was sure he was going to proposition me.

"I want to be a girl just like you," he told me. "You're beautiful. Could we be friends?" I guess it was a kind of proposition after all.

Teru seemed to have some time on his hands, so I brought him up to speed with what'd been going on. Was he surprised! I could imagine his eyes, with their green contact lenses he's so into now, wide open. I love his eyes. They're different from most Japanese eyes, or men's or young people's eyes. More like the weird eyes of some alien from outer space. Like on that commercial, you know? I think it was for ACOM?

So, anyway, I didn't like Teru as a guy, but I still wanted to watch him all the time. It's like when I see him I feel calm, unafraid. Most guys want to get it on—you don't know what they're going to do to you and deep down that scares me. Maybe I don't really trust them. But Teru is kind, more fragile than Toshi and the others, and a very good guy. His kind of hurt-by-the-world look is cute. Teru's into role-playing, and I love that part of him, too. I don't think he's been doing it lately—it's too hot—but this spring he was always dressed up like characters from *Battle Royale*. He'd wear a school uniform with one of those high, round collars.

"Kirarin, do you mean that murder that was in all the papers yesterday? Is this the same guy who beat his mother to death and ran away?"

Teru seemed worried about being overheard and kept his voice down.

"That's the one. He lives next door to Toshi. At first he stole Toshi's cell phone and bicycle and took off. He's a weird guy, and started calling all the girls listed in her contacts. Yuzan seemed to like him so she helped him, gave him a bike and new cell phone. He called me, too. When I dialed the number the guy was so happy and said he'd like to meet up with me."

"But why would Yuzan help him out?"

"I think because her mother is dead, too. It made her sympathize with him. He called me, too, but I just led him on."

"That's pretty risky, Kirarin," Teru said, sounding worried. "That kid must be pretty desperate by now."

But would a desperate guy sound like one of those horny guys who e-mail me?

"I don't think so," I said. "It's more like he feels free and ready to get it on."

"What are you thinking? It's *terrible*." Teru sounded more like a girl than me. "And why does he want to meet you? Why not Toshi, Yuzan, or Terauchi?"

Teru'd never met any of them, but I'd told him all about them.

"Maybe 'cause I used my cute voice. Like always."

Teru didn't like it that I played around in online chat rooms. Everybody just tells lies on those sites, he said, all serious, so what's the fun in that? I knew that but still held out the slim hope that I might actually hook up with some hot guy. That slim hope always drove me to the sites. Maybe I'm boy crazy or something.

"This is sounding worse and worse."

"But how many chances do you get to meet an actual murderer?"

"Mmm," Teru said, thinking it over.

"Yeah, I suppose," he said. "Let me think about this and get back to you during lunch. See ya."

I was thinking about getting Toshi's advice, too, and was about to press the speed dial, but decided against it. I could always depend on her, but I knew she'd get all serious on me. She didn't really understand me that well.

Of the four of us in our group I'm the only one who isn't a virgin. I'm also the only one who has made other friends, people I go out with outside of school. The only one who posts all kinds of lies on online chat rooms, the only one who has a gay friend. The other three girls, though, just think I'm a cute, cheerful, what-you-see-is-what-you-get type of girl. When Toshi told me that just looking at me calms her down, that made me feel all squirmy. I'm not deliberately trying to fool them, it's just that I'm not as simple as they think.

The other group I'm in is a bunch of girls who do a just-okay job of studying for college exams, figure they'll get into some easy junior college, and love to party. Girls who, when the time comes, will marry some so-so guy, raise some kids, and continue to shop and have fun like they did when they were single. They're very matter-of-fact about going out with guys, and just let life take care of itself. They don't smoke, but carry Zippo lighters and when a guy takes out a cigarette, they love to say, "I have a lighter. How 'bout I give you a light?" All they think about is how to please guys.

So, anyway, I'd go with these girls to Shibuya, get picked up by guys, go with them to a karaoke place, go drinking, spend the whole night having fun. If I run across a guy I like, I might go to a hotel with him, but I absolutely never do it for money. Once a guy finds out you're selling it, his attitude does a one-eighty. I like fooling around with guys, but hate being used like a toy. That makes me sad and miserable. Fooling around with guys is thrilling, like walking next to a busy highway. If you fall off the curb, it's all over.

Teru never says anything about me playing around with guys. I think maybe he's jealous, wanting to do the same himself. Gay guys like regular guys, just like girls. In that sense it's a shame that we can't go to Shibuya together and get picked up, 'cause we get along so well.

I'm in these two groups because I feel like I belong right in the middle between them. Toshi, Terauchi, and Yuzan are nice girls, but they're so serious sometimes I feel like I can't breathe. I feel kind of on edge, like I've always got to say something clever or they'll make fun of me. Which doesn't mean I think the same way as the other group, that you can kind of just muddle through life. I want to study and get into a decent college and get a good job. When it comes time to marry, it's got to be somebody I really like, and my partner's got to love me most of all. That said, this is the best time of my life, so I figure I'd better enjoy it and not get all hung up on the consequences.

Two other girls in this Good Times group are in the same year as me in school. They come to school with dyed hair and makeup, like they're announcing the fact that they're out for a good time. They figure if they flaunt it, the guys will flock to them. I find this all kind of courageous and their flirtiness kind of sneaky. I'm more the serious and "healthy" sexy high school girl—which, I guess, makes me courageous and sneaky, too. We want to get guys to pay attention to us, and when we're together we help each other stand out. That's probably why we get along so well. When I run across those girls at school, though, they don't say anything to me. We pretend to be strangers and signal each other with glances. If we have something we want to talk about, we do it by cell phone or text message. It's a secret relationship, in other words.

So the friends I can meet in front of everyone are Toshi, Ter-auchi, and Yuzan—our little foursome—but it's much more complicated than that, 'cause I have underground roots branching out in lots of directions. What I talk about changes depending on the type of friends I'm with.

The Good Time girls never talk about the future or anything even remotely serious. It's clothes, makeup, and guys, twenty-four/seven. With Toshi, Terauchi, and Yuzan I can talk about school, college, but when it comes to discussing guys, I can't talk with them, and don't want to, either. So each group is kind of one-sided. I guess Teru's the one who overlaps with both.

Teru says he can relax with me 'cause he doesn't see me as the opposite sex. We're such good friends that, like I said before, we even joke about pretending to be married, but Teru said if we did that he'd worry about what'd happen if we were both after the same guy. That'll never happen, I told him. That kind of situation would only make both of us unhappy, so I'd never do it. "You wouldn't do it, either, right?" I insisted, and got him to promise. I did this because when I was a freshman I had a terrible experience. A guy betrayed me.

There was this guy I was crazy about. I could talk about everything with him—what I wanted to be when I was older, problems I was having, even chatty stuff like clothes and hairstyles. Talking with him made me feel free, like all the bad things about me didn't matter and everything was on a positive track. As long as he was with me I felt like I didn't need girlfriends for the rest of my life. Maybe I never would have become friends with Teru, either. But he slept with another high school girl and when I found out we fought and split up.

When I think about him now I get all sad and teary. I guess I really did love him. When we were having sex, I could barely keep myself from yelling out, "I love you! I love you!" Still, getting stabbed in the back like that was the first crushing experience I've ever had. I'm sure Toshi and the others have never experienced that. When things were going well with that guy, I felt completely superior, like I was a grown-up woman. And I wish I could get that feeling back.

One time when we were eating lunch together I asked the other girls for their advice. I was desperate and wanted see what my three serious friends might have to say about the situation.

"I have this friend," I began, "and she's going out with a boy from a city high school. She says he's a senior and pretty busy studying for college entrance exams, but he's also in a band, plays

soccer, does everything well, and is cute, too. This girl says they
really get along well and have even exchanged rings."

Terauchi plunged in at this point: "How far have they gone?"

Toshi answered for me. "Of course they've done it. They've
exchanged rings and everything."

"Dude. By getting along do you mean sex?"

"I guess so."

"You mean they're compatible size-wise?"

"Or maybe like how passionate they are?"

After Terauchi and Toshi finished their little dialogue, they
looked at me. They were very intuitive, so I had to watch my step.
I went on, hiding my confusion.

"So, anyway, the guy slept with another girl. And my friend just
can't forgive him, and it's really hard on her. The guy says he was
just having a fling, it didn't mean anything, that she's the only one
he loves. But my friend can't believe him. It's really tough on her,
she's so miserable she feels like her chest is going to rip apart, so
she can't forgive him. She asked for my advice about what she
should do, but I have no idea what to tell her."

Toshi had this weird look on her face. "How did she find out he
was having an affair? Did she catch them in the act, like in a
drama?"

"There were tons of gushy e-mails on his cell phone from the
other girl. About fifty every day."

"So you're saying this 'friend' of yours checked her boyfriend's
cell phone."

The best I could do was nod. "That's what she told me."

"That sucks," Toshi declared. "Checking somebody's else's cell
phone really sucks."

"But if she really loves him, don't you think she might do something like that?"

I was on the verge of crying. Toshi looked surprised but went on vaguely: "Well, you could be right. That might happen, I suppose. I don't know, I never liked any guy that much."

Taking a sip from her water bottle, Terauchi made a sour face. "If this friend can't forgive him for the affair, why doesn't she just forget about him? There're lots of other guys out there."

"Sure there are other guys out there," I said, "but my friend loves *him*. So what do you expect? She got worried and checked out his text messages. She loves him so much—that's why she's in agony wondering whether she should forgive him or not."

"What she should do is forgive him, for the time being, then make some prank calls to the other girl to get back at her. Payback."

Up to this point, Yuzan hadn't said a word, so when she muttered this I was shocked. I'd already done what she suggested a long time ago.

"That's an idea. I'll pass it along," I said.

"I don't think she should do that. It'll just make her feel dirty, and she'll hate herself." Toshi shook her head. She always comes up with the right answer. She was absolutely right. I was already struggling with a guilty conscience. When I told the other girl she was ugly, she yelled back this: "You idiot! You're just angry 'cause I stole Wataru away from you!" So it was obvious I'd called her out of jealousy. It was like having mud thrown all over my face. And that mud is still there, plastered on.

Terauchi shrugged, agreeing with Toshi, and the three of them went back to eating their lunches like they'd had enough of the topic. It hit me right at that instant that they knew I'd been sleeping around with guys.

When I told all this to Teru, he held my hand and said, "You must have felt awful, Kirarin. Your pride got in the way then and you couldn't be honest. Pride's such a pain in the butt. Who needs it, anyway?"

"You're right, I did feel awful. I didn't know what to do. I was so stubborn I made a fool of myself. Maybe I should have just put up with it, but I couldn't. I-I want to see him! I still love him. . . ."

I burst out crying at this point, and after I had a good cry I felt better. I needed a friend like Teru, someone who could sympathize with me. My three girlfriends and I might get along, but they just kept on growing up, unaware of the pain I was feeling. I think that whole incident changed me, but to them I was still the same old Kirarin: cheerful, cute, well raised. And we were all going to grow up and this gap between who I really was and their perception of me was never going to be bridged. Friends are a weird thing. It seems like they know all about you, but then they don't understand you at all. Maybe Teru is the friend I really need, but since he's a guy, at least biologically, I feel like someday even he might betray me. Maybe deep down I just don't trust guys.

I lost my virginity when I was a sophomore in junior high. It's embarrassing, actually, to use a phrase like "lose my virginity." The whole act was meaningless. I don't even remember what the guy looked like. He was a student at a private high school and had dyed reddish brown hair. Sometimes when I remember him it makes me feel depressed, wondering why I did it with a guy like that. He was a rude, stupid guy who liked to lecture me on how girls should act. They shouldn't lounge around naked, they shouldn't smoke, et cetera.

Ever since then I can tell right away if a guy's a moron: like if, during sex, he's not gentle with me. It's weird, but there's like a law that idiocy and kindness are in inverse proportion. If, for instance, a guy goes into a club and goes straight to the back to sit down—you're talking moron. When he's doing karaoke and insists on selecting only the songs he likes—another moron. Guys who go out to pick up girls are morons, too, 'cause they're so self-centered. So why do I like to be picked up, then? I can't figure it out. Sometimes I think how great it would be if Terauchi and Toshi and I could discuss all this, but Toshi's too serious and Terauchi is too good at hiding who she really is, so I just can't bring myself to open up to them.

Yuzan, though, is different. Sometimes I feel like asking her advice. But I know she's a lesbian. Her feelings are different from those of a girl like me.

When we went on our school trip sophomore year in high school, we got hold of some whiskey. Yuzan got drunk and crawled into bed with me. When I screamed, she said, "I'm just pretending to sneak into a lover's room!" and tried to explain it away. But her eyes were serious. She must have regretted getting wasted and letting her secret out, 'cause in the middle of the night I saw her crying. Ever since then I've sympathized with her. Since she doesn't have a Good Times group to play around with like I do, she doesn't have an outlet for her feelings. She should just come out and let everybody know, like Teru did. And have a guy as a friend.

It was after one when Teru finally called me. The train was pretty empty, so I went over to the door and we had a long, whispered conversation. The AC blows hard next to the door and I was freezing. My teeth were chattering.

"I was thinking about it," he said, "and I don't think you should go."

"I'm already on the train."

I was riding the Takasaki Line out of Ueno. It was just like when I go to see my online friends. I go out because I'm curious about who I'll meet. For fun. Just a game to kill time. When I get to the arranged meeting place, I stand off to one side, dial the guy's number, and figure out which one he is. I check him out and if I don't like what I see, then I go home. If the guy looks okay, then I go over and say hello. Most of the time it's a bust. It's kind of fun, though, to see through their lies. It's even more interesting with Worm, since he's a murderer. I want to watch him from a distance for a while.

Teru sounded betrayed. "I can't believe it. Why are you doing this, Kirarin? To get to Kumagaya you need to take the Jōetsu Shinkansen, don't you? Why are you doing this?"

"I'm not on the Shinkansen. I'm taking the Takasaki Line."

"But it's a long way away, isn't it? Why go all the way out there?"

"The guy's a murderer. Wouldn't *you* like to meet him?"

Teru was silent for a while, and finally replied: "I feel sorry for this guy—Worm? But I don't want to see him or have anything to do with him. And I can't figure out why you'd want to. You sound like one of those stupid talk shows."

I like Teru a lot because he can give these kinds of serious replies. And I respect him, too. Still, I had to see Worm with my own eyes.

"Maybe I don't even know why myself," I said, and stopped. "Maybe I wanted to feel superior to Toshi and Terauchi, too."

"You already do," Teru said calmly.

"No, I don't."

"Yes, you do. Because you're part of a hidden world that doesn't include them. Because you have me, a gay guy, as a friend. Because you hook up with guys. Am I right?"

He was on the right track, but it wasn't exactly like that. I thought I knew about guys, but I really didn't. I should have stayed longer with that guy who betrayed me. It was like there was a door there, and no matter how hard or awful it was, I should have opened it and stepped into another world. Then I would have been able to understand him. But I got angry, slammed the door shut, and ran away. Toshi and Terauchi might not be like me, since I only know guys in a shallow way; when the time comes, I think they'd be a lot stronger. They would have opened the door. Which gives me kind of an inferiority complex.

"Sorry if I went too far," Teru continued, "but I'm worried about you. Do you want me to meet you there?"

"No, you can't do that. You're working."

"It's okay. I can take off early."

I hung up, then sat down in an empty seat and gazed out the window at the endless stream of houses passing by. The roofs of the houses lined up on the west side glittered in the hot summer sun. If you were looking down from an airplane, it would be even more dazzlingly bright. I have to be strong enough to reflect back light myself, but why do I go out at night to Shibuya and play around, why do I go on those online chat rooms? I know that relationships with guys are superficial, but still I do it. Complicated relationships with friends just wear me out. Why can't I just be strong and simple? Thoughts like these get me a little depressed.

When I got to Kumagaya, I went straight to the restroom. I might go home without actually meeting him, 'cause I was afraid he'd be disappointed when he saw me. It'd be annoying, too, if I found out I'd been fooled. My face was sweaty, so I wiped it with my handkerchief and redid my eyebrows. I checked my pink T-shirt for sweat stains, spritzed on some more deodorant. Only after these preparations did I phone Worm from inside the station.

"Where are you?" he said. "I'm at the station."

The guy's pretty fast. I hadn't expected him to be there already. I was startled and looked around for a place to hide. I had to check

him out first, to see what kind of guy he was, otherwise there was
no way I was going to meet him. I circled back behind the kiosks
and looked around the station to see if there were any high
school–age guys on cell phones.

"How are you dressed?"

"What kind of clothes do *you* have on, Kirarin?"

"You tell me first."

"No, you first."

What the— The guy must be hidden somewhere himself, trying
to check me out first. Just what you'd expect from a criminal. But
he was no match for me when it came to maneuvering on the
phone.

"I'm wearing a bright red swimsuit," I said boldly, "and black
high heels, and I'm carrying a huge Louis Vuitton bag."

"Pretty gaudy outfit. I'm dressed like an old-time Japanese soldier. I've got a cap on, and gaiters, even in this awful heat. I'm a
private. I have a carved wooden rifle, too, not a real one, though,
'cause that'd be dangerous."

A Japanese soldier? What a jerk. I stifled a laugh. My eyes kept
moving, scanning the people walking through the station. Young
part-timers, grade school kids, a middle-aged lady, high school
girls, station employees, married couples. But not any guy who
looked like he was in high school.

"What do you mean, a carved wooden rifle?" I asked.

"What kind of swimsuit do you have on? A bikini?"

"Sorry, but it's one of those school one-piece swimsuits. You can
tell 'cause it's got a nametag on the chest. It says 'Higashiyama.' "

"A school swimsuit, huh?" he said, his tone changed. "You're
just screwing with my head, aren't you?"

I got flustered since he was right on target. How did you know
that, Worm?

"No, I'm not."

"Really? Experienced guys who target young girls like those school swimsuits. It's obscene. So you know what that kind of guys like?"

"Whatever. Where are you?" I asked.

"Where are *you*, babe?"

So it was no more "Kirarin," but "babe"? He was making fun of me, and I didn't like it one bit.

"Who gave you the right to call me that?"

"Enough with the attitude. You want to meet me, right? Want to check me out? 'Cause I'm a murderer on the run. Babes like you enjoy checking me out. Put it on your blog, right? I know the type."

"If that's what's you think, fine by me. 'Cause I'm out of here."

"Suit yourself. I'm leaving, too."

"How can you leave when I came all this way? Okay, have it your way—I'm going to go into a police station and tell them the boy they're looking for is right around the corner. Give them your cell phone number, too."

There'd been this echo like he was inside somewhere, but now I sensed he was leaving. His breathing got a little ragged, so I knew he was walking. I heard the sound of cars. Sounded like Worm was exiting the station. I stretched, looking outside, but didn't spot him.

"We don't have to meet today," he said. "I'm out of here. Sorry."

The phone clicked dead. It made me so angry. He wasn't just going to leave me like this after asking me to come, was he? After all the money I'd spent on train fare? I ran outside, completely ignoring my ironclad rule about not pursuing things too far. There was a line of taxis outside the station, but no people. It was so steamy out that everyone was staying inside. I stood there, blankly,

outside this nearly deserted entrance of the station. He wasn't anywhere around. I'd been *this close* to seeing him. An oddly dry wind
was blowing, messing up my long hair. My body had been cooled
down by the AC inside, but now my arms and legs were getting
hot. My back was all sweaty.

"That's not a swimsuit," a voice said from behind me.

Damn, he got me, I thought, my head getting hotter than the
temperature outside. More than anything I hated to lose the game.
Worm must have been watching me from a distance, thinking,
This is Kirarin, checking me out before he made his move. Just
like I do to guys.

I slowly turned around. This guy smiling at me was tall and
thin, but terribly stooped over. Gone was the challenging attitude
on the phone. He was totally casual now. I'd pictured Worm as
this haunted-looking, sweaty, smelly guy, confused and saddened
by what he'd done. But the real Worm was tanned and healthy-
looking. He looked neat and tidy, with a clean white T-shirt on and
oversize black shorts. Hoisting a dusty backpack. His hair was
disheveled, cowlicks everywhere. Could he really have killed his
own mother? He looked like some local high school kid on his way
to cram school. I stood there, vacantly looking at Worm's face,
dizzy with the heat and frustration at having lost the game.

"So you're Kirarin. You're not like Toshi or Yuzan at all."

"Really? I don't know about that."

"Come on, you know what I'm talking about. You play around
with guys. I can tell by your face."

"I don't play around," I said.

"You're cute, but tough."

"No, I'm not."

I scrunched up my lips and made a sulky face, turning into flirty
me. I like nothing better than to twist guys around my little finger,

but when I meet a guy I turn all passive. Which might be because, like I said, I basically don't trust guys. I hate it—here I am acting all flirty even with a criminal. Teru, get here quick! I thought. This guy's the overbearing type I can't deal with. What if he murders me?! Kind of calculating of me to rely on Teru, though . . .

"You're not really going to go to the police, are you?" Worm asked.

"I just said that 'cause all of a sudden you said you were leaving."

"Why are you lying? Lying's a waste of energy." Worm watched me, a hand held up to shield his eyes from the sun shining behind me. "Anyway, it's too hot—why don't we find someplace cooler to talk."

Worm pulled a cap out of his back pocket, put it on, and set off down the street.

"Wait a second—what did you do with Yuzan's bike?"

"I threw it away and grabbed another one."

"You shouldn't just throw it away, it's hers. Don't you feel bad?"

Worm glanced back at me, his eyes fixed.

"Nah, I think it's okay. It's an emergency. I'm in a war. So I don't have time to think about things like that. The whole country, all one hundred million people, is in an uproar about this high school student who whacked his mother."

I was wondering how such a skinny guy could have done it, killed his mom. They said he beat her to death, but with puny arms like that, could he really have killed a woman all by himself? What would it feel like to murder somebody, anyway? And your own mother? I was scared of Worm, but at the same time I had all kinds of questions I wanted to ask him. Worm pointed to a mall just ahead.

"That should be cool, let's go there."

As I followed after him I looked all around me like some gawking tourist. I felt okay, though, since I figured he wouldn't dare kill me in a crowded mall. Worm motioned with his chin toward a bargain store.

"When I heard you were coming I washed up in the swimming pool and bought a new T-shirt and boxers in the store over there. Four hundred eighty yen for the shirt and three hundred for the underwear."

"How much money do you have on you?"

"Not much. I started out with twenty thousand, but I've used it all."

"What on?"

But Worm didn't reply.

"Finding food and a place to sleep isn't so tough, but what's hardest is taking a bath. There aren't many public baths around, and even if I found one they probably wouldn't let me in 'cause I'm too filthy. So it's a real headache. Now I know why homeless old guys stink so much. They won't let 'em into public baths. If I could solve that problem I could keep running forever."

"You wouldn't be able to run away for the rest of your life."

"Yeah? You really think so?"

Worm spun around and faced me. His eyes were sharp, penetrating, and he looked pretty intelligent. I remembered my old boyfriend, the one I was so crazy about who stabbed me in the back. His eyes looked like this, too, sometimes. From way down inside me, hatred still boiled up. I *hate* him, I really do. The guy who made me suffer. Since I was quiet, Worm went on.

"Why do you think I won't be able to run away?"

"Why don't you try it, then, if you think you can?"

"I'm going to."

"But you couldn't your whole life. I mean, you're only seventeen, right?"

"You probably think you're going to have a long life."

I froze.

"Yeah, I do," I replied.

"That all depends on the person."

Worm went into the mall ahead of me. It was a huge one, with a movie theater inside. In the middle of the building was some sort of sculpture that was supposed to be angels all intertwined, I guess, and around it were benches filled with high school couples making out. I bought a can of iced tea from a nearby vending machine. I thought about it for a bit, then sprang for a can for Worm, too. He'd long since plunked himself down on one of the benches and accepted the can of tea from me like he'd been expecting it all along.

"I don't think any of these people would believe me if I told them I killed my mother. It's amazing they kept my photo out of the media. It's all over the Internet, though. Do you use the Internet?"

"On my phone, yeah," I said, flashing him my clamshell phone. "That's about it. I don't own a computer."

The couple next to us stopped kissing and, hand in hand, walked off, so I used this chance to ask him what I'd been wanting to know. "Why did you kill your mother?"

"I forget why. Reasons don't matter, anyway. I just got pissed off. What's more important is how an experience makes you go off to another world, how you live your life there. In that other world. And what you think about the world you left behind. Know what I mean?"

" 'Know what I mean?' Stop acting so stuck-up."

Worm stared at me in surprise.

"It's strange that girls like guys who act all big and then get angry about it. Kind of inconsistent, if you ask me."

"I'd think it's strange if it wasn't."

To tell the truth, I liked talking like this. It got me excited. Sure, Worm wasn't that appealing on the outside, but he did think about all sorts of things. And more than that, he was a guy who'd killed his mother, who'd seen this "other world," so talking with him kept me on my toes. I was wondering how far my experiences would take me in a sparring match with him. This was another kind of game.

"So you're never going back home?" I asked him.

"I was thinking about going back. How I'd need money to get back. But I won't do that until after I've run away some more. It'd be a waste if I don't experience being on the run some more."

Worm stretched out his skinny legs and gazed up at the ceiling. The domed ceiling had a stained-glass picture on it depicting most of the city, and the midsummer sun tinted the white floor in dark-ish, dirty colors.

"Why would you go home?"

"I want to kill my old man," he said, shooting me a glance. "How about you? Anybody you feel like killing?"

I thought it over for a while. I wouldn't mind killing *that* jerk, the guy who destroyed my trust in men. I wonder what he's doing now. The sadness and frustration I felt when he betrayed me changed me forever. He just split, leaving me behind, never the same again.

"Well, I guess there is."

"Why do you want to kill him? 'Cause his existence makes you suffer, right? 'Cause you'd be better off if he wasn't alive?"

"I don't know. . . ." I said, tilting my head. "I'd like it if he died, but what I'd really like is to get revenge on him, make him suffer, make him regret he did a stupid thing like betraying a great girl like me."

"Nah, that's too wishy-washy. You have to make him totally vanish from the face of the earth. Otherwise, if he's still alive, you won't ever get rid of the darkness that's in your heart."

"But killing him will make that even worse, won't it?"

"No. You're saying that 'cause the darkness in your heart isn't that deep. The deeper that darkness gets, the more you have to get rid of it. No matter what."

Worm was so weird. He was starting to scare me.

"Aren't you sad that your mother died? And you're the one who killed her? Don't you feel sorry for her?"

Just then my cell phone rang. It was Teru.

"Kirarin? Where are you? Are you okay?"

"I'm fine. I'm in a mall in front of the station."

"I'm going to get on the Takasaki Line pretty soon. I'll call you when I get there."

So Teru was coming to be with me. Relieved, I opened my bag to put away my cell phone. Worm reached out and grabbed the phone away.

"The army's requisitioning this."

"Stop it. What do you think you're doing?"

I tried to grab it back, but he stuffed it in his pocket. Desperately, I looked around. There were two young mothers nearby with small children. They were smiling at us, probably thinking we were a couple having a little spat. No! I wanted to scream. This guy's nuts! He's the guy who beat his mother to death. He's running away on a bike. How could I make them understand the situation? I stood up, thinking I'd find a security guard, but Worm grabbed my arm and pulled me back. He held both my arms tight and looked into my eyes.

"Kirarin, you really like me, don't you?"

"You've gotta be kidding. No way."

"I'll make you like me. Come on."

What the hell did he mean? I didn't know how to react. Pulling me by the arm, Worm headed for the exit.

"You told somebody you were going to meet me, didn't you? You came to see me 'cause you wanted to see something scary, so why don't we get changed together? I can make you into a new person. And we'll wipe the smug smile off your old boyfriend's face."

"How're we going to do that?"

As I said this, I was thinking there was nothing in the world I'd rather do.

"We'll do some bad things together. Then we'll go back to Tokyo and kill my old man. And I'll take you to a whole different world."

A whole different world. The world that lay just beyond that door I never could open. It was appealing and frightening, all at the same time. Worm stamped hard on the welcome mat at the entrance of the mall and the cheap automatic doors slid open. My skin was hit by the blazing heat outside.

"Okay—first we gotta grab a cab."

"Where are we going?"

"We're near the Nakasendo Highway and that goes to Karui-zawa. It's nice and cool there."

"I thought you said you don't have any money."

"It won't cost anything. I'm tired of riding around on a bike."

"But it won't work."

"Well, check this out. I bought a knife." Worm shook his back-pack proudly. "Paid ten thousand yen for it. Totally sharp."

So he was planning on hijacking a cab.

"I don't think you should do that."

"How come?"

Worm stood still and looked at me. He had that metallic, rusty sort of smell that young guys have. Sometimes there's a guy like that among the ones who try to pick me up in Shibuya. They're always the ones who are dying to have sex. With Worm, though, it isn't sex so much as some other desire that's driving him. Something I can't figure out. Still, I remembered that guys with a smell like that didn't particularly turn me off.

The first thing I heard was a woman's whispered laugh. And then I opened my eyes and saw some heavy, dingy green curtains. The same crummy curtains my old lady had bought at Peacock for my room, so at first I was sure I was back in my house. It was the first time I'd slept in a bed in days and I'd slept so soundly my memory had flown away. I totally forgot that I'd beaten my mother to death; to me, at that moment, the old lady was just an annoying woman I had to put up with. I was positive she'd slipped into my room while I was asleep and was whispering something. Shut the hell up! Get *outta* here! The old lady, after all, was the only woman I was close to, so I figured it had to be her.

"No, I'm fine. Believe me."

But it wasn't my mother talking. It was the girl I'd just met, this high school girl who went by this kind of embarrassing nickname. Finally the memory came back to me—my mother was dead. Thank God, I thought, she's no longer in this world. She's vanished forever. I was so relieved I started to laugh, silently. The skin from my cheek to my chin was wet. I was flustered at first, thinking I must have been crying in my sleep, but it turned out to be drool. I quietly wiped it all away with the back of my hand, pretending to remain asleep while I listened in on Kirarin's conversation. I had no idea what this girl was thinking, why she would want to be with me. As head of military affairs, I should have done a better job of investigating my opponent's mind-set beforehand. Why I should know a term like "head of military affairs," I had no idea, but I knew everything now. Ever since I was riding my bike, trying to stay awake, the spirit of that tortured Japanese soldier was with me.

"I understand that you're worried, Teru, but I'm fine. I'm okay.

I appreciate your worrying about me, I really do. He's kind of weird, but interesting. I mean, when we met at the station we were arguing about what we were wearing. And he insisted he was dressed like an army private. Kind of crazy, right? A weird guy. But I don't think he's going to hurt me. I don't know why, but I feel sure of that. So you can go home. I won't tell you where we are. It's a love hotel. What? No, we're not doing it. No way! I wouldn't do it with a guy like that. Yeah, okay. I'll call you if that happens. Just don't worry. I've hung out with guys in Shibuya, so I'll be okay. And you know what? He's made me want to get revenge. No, not on my mother. On Wataru. The guy who did those horrible things to me. I loved Wataru, that's why I let him come inside me. And then he went and slept with another girl, the bastard. And a complete idiot, no less. When I realized he did it 'cause he looked down on me, I couldn't forgive him. This was more than a year ago, but it still makes me totally depressed. I'm thinking of meeting him, and killing him. I feel *dark*. *Dark* Kirarin. Not the cute, cheerful Kirarin everybody's used to. But it feels good, somehow. You know what I mean? You really do? This is the first time I ever felt like taking revenge on someone. It makes me feel great, happy like never before. So anyway, wait, huh? Yeah, you're right. Even the way I speak's gotten a little tougher. . . ."

Kirarin gave a small sigh and hung up, ending her call with this Teru guy. She immediately started calling someone else. No doubt Yuzan or Toshi or Terauchi, one of her dumb group of friends. She was leaving a message. While I was asleep she must have stolen back the phone I requisitioned. The girl was more formidable than I imagined.

"Hi, it's me, Kirarin. Call me, don't send a text message. Something really big's happening and I want to tell you about it. See ya."

I got out of bed and yanked open the curtains. Beyond the rice field outside there was another love hotel much like this one. It was supposed to be like some European castle, though with a huge dome on top. And on top of that, there was a large orange crescent moon. Kind of surreal. Like a sickle stuck in the head of Atsushi Ōnita, the pro wrestler. I felt excited, like when Ōnita and Mr. Pogo are getting it on in the ring. I got all worked up looking at it.

"You slept really well. You were snoring."

Kirarin hurriedly ended her call and said this in a sweet nasal voice. All of a sudden, I had this stupid memory of how I used to dream of a younger sister. There was a guy in our school who wrote his own porno manga and used to bring them to school, and he'd always have a young girl character in the story who calls the hero "Brother!" And of course this "older brother" commands his "little sister" to take off her school uniform and then takes his time while he enjoys violating her. The girl protests but removes her own panties. How stupid. The guy who wrote this is a superbrain, the kind you know could get into Tokyo University Law Department, so it's kind of amazing how predictable his manga always were. What really makes me laugh is how when he used to read his manga aloud to everybody he always used this sweet voice for the young girl character. "Brother—please don't punish me! I'm scared!" My point is that Kirarin's voice was just like the voice that guy used when he acted out the young girl character from his manga. And it made me really pissed.

I don't need a younger sister. I don't need any women at all. I've been *transformed*. Maybe because I took a bath after we checked into this love hotel. As soon as my salt suit was washed away I completed my new personality. The soul of the former Japanese soldier.

I used to be way hornier than most guys. When we lived in that condo, I liked the young wife next door; I listened in on their love-making and even stole her panties. And after we moved, I enjoyed peeping in on Toshi. But not anymore. I was really happy at my transformation—or evolution, you might say. I had to change, or else I couldn't steel myself for battle. So I cautioned Kirarin in no uncertain terms.

"Knock it off with that anime voice."

"Well, excuse *me*," she said, her face all gloomy. "But that's my normal voice."

"No, it isn't. When you're flirting with guys, your voice changes. That's a part of you I'll take care of, you can count on it. And who said you could use the phone, anyway?" I grabbed the phone back from her and shoved it in my pants pocket. "It's been requisitioned by the military. And you stole it. You looking to go into the brig?"

"*Brig?* What are you talking about, you idiot?"

Kirarin turned away, angry. Her expression was still flirty, though—I could tell. She was getting a thrill being with me, the murderer. What a flirt.

"Nothing stupid about it. Are you going to follow orders or what?"

"No way. Who the heck do you think you are, anyway?" she complained. I didn't like the way her lips stuck out when she spoke. It was pornographic. Now that I'd done my mother in, I had to mow down all the rest of the pornographic women in the world. Somebody's got to give the order. I glanced around the room, looking for an officer. But no one was there.

"Stop talking like that."

"How can you say that?" she said. "You make me so angry. Who paid for this hotel, anyway? You said you wanted to go to Karui-zawa, but you were getting so sleepy you almost passed out on the street. I should have just left you. Without me, they wouldn't have let you stay here. Maybe I shouldn't have been so nice to you."

"I collapsed because it was a long, hard march."

"You're schizo, you know that?"

Kirarin laughed shrilly. Her laughter hurt my ears, and I wanted to rip my head off. The reality came to me—I'm alone on the front line, the only one still fighting the war. Before that old Filipino man and woman can torture me, I've got to escape into the jungle. And regroup for the next battle. My war has just begun. That's the world I'm in—*my* world. And I have to train this woman to be a combatant, as soon as possible. 'Cause I'm the veteran soldier.

"Hey there, recruit! Suck me."

I said it just to harass her, but my penis started to visibly harden.

"Are you crazy? No way." Kirarin brushed my hand aside with unexpected force and escaped to a corner of the room. "You're the worst. Something's wrong with you, you know that?"

"Of course it is. I wasted my old lady. I ran after her like this and smacked her a good one right in the head with my bat. Could you have done that?"

I snatched up a pillow and swung it around hard, like it was a bat. Fuzz and strands of hair and pubic hairs flew all over the place. Kirarin stared at the pillow, then at me, like she'd never seen such a gross sight in her life.

"No way I could do that," she said. "I like my mom."

"What about your dad, then?"

"My dad? That I might consider," Kirarin said, her gaze suddenly flitting about the room. "My dad's a totally cold person. When I was in junior high, we got this call late at night. When I picked up, a woman was on the other end and said, 'Are you there, Daddy? If you are, give it to me. I'm gonna die.' Is that the kind of thing you should say to a child? I don't think so. I was so pissed. Go ahead and die, why don't you, I thought. But I was still little, so I went and woke up my father. I was careful to make sure Mom didn't find out. And Dad just pretended to be asleep and ignored me. So this is the kind of man he is, I thought—pitiful. I felt sorry for the woman, but one of them was as bad as the other. And I started to hate my mother, too, since she'd chosen this kind of guy to marry. I went through a stage where I was angry and distrusted all adults. I hate all you jerks, I thought. Especially my father. Many times I felt like killing him. But I don't care anymore. I don't feel like murdering him. 'Cause I'm old enough to do whatever I like on my own now. That's why I think you were wrong. You went too far. I really feel sorry for your mother, you know. You're going to suffer the rest of your life."

This declaration of hers really pissed me off. My life proceeds at a different speed from other people's. This is kind of an out-of-date way of putting it, but ever since the murder I've been *turbo-charged*. I'm free to change my world any way I want to. No more being told what to do, having people lay a guilt trip on me. I'm in control. I'm the commander in charge of the battle to create my world. Still, Kirarin's attitude made me uneasy.

"Pretty sure of yourself, aren't you?" I said. "You didn't grab my weapon by any chance, did you?"

I rummaged around in my backpack, which I'd put next to my bed. The butcher knife I'd just bought had to be inside. My tool to kill them all before they get to me—before that scrawny old coot hauls me out to the main square and drop-kicks me, before the old hag spits all over me, before they bash me over the head with a hammer. The knife was still flat inside its box. Kirarin was covering her mouth with her hand, but she was clearly sneering at how upset I'd got.

She doesn't get it. I suddenly realized this. This girl *just doesn't get it*. I'm in the middle of a war and she doesn't give a damn.

Which is why she's laughing. She just came to see me in the midst of battle. She, and all her little friends, are just having a ball observing me. You're right. I killed my old lady. And I'll probably cry about it the rest of my life. But enough with your cheap sympathy—I don't need it. I got even angrier.

"If you think I'm weird, then get out of here! I'm not some public show for you."

"Hmm—so you *can* be serious if you want to."

"I *am* serious."

I wanted to threaten her a bit, so I pulled the knife out of the box. I held on to the black handle and swooshed the knife around a couple of times. The butcher knife was long and sharp and scary-looking. I looked around for something to use so I could hang it around my waist, but all I could see was the belt to the bathrobe. That would look stupid, so I gave up the idea. Kirarin remained in a corner, frozen. But her eyes showed a lot of respect. Or maybe fear? Doesn't matter. Anyway, this was the second time I saw a woman look this confused. I remembered how Mom looked when she saw me swing a bat at her, an awful feeling to remember. The instant she realized her whole world was crumbling around her. Or maybe she was repenting for how badly she'd treated me. At any rate, her face reflected the chaos that had overtaken her.

My mom was definitely at fault. She was guilty of creating a history between us, a past that justified me putting her in her place. Guilty of leading me around by the nose, messing up my life, revealing my secrets to the world. I was a colony and she was the occupying force. She created the rubber plantation, made me work from dawn to night, then took away the whole harvest for herself. A colony where everything was plundered. I don't know what exactly was stolen from me. But most definitely the old lady continued to steal *something*. In Kirarin's case, there was no reason yet to get rid of her. Being slutty wasn't enough of a reason. I lowered the butcher knife. I'm still sane. Not crazy yet.

"I'm trying to help," she said. "So stop threatening me."

Even from a distance I could see that tears were welling up in her eyes. Hey, I thought you respected me. Finding it all kinds of strange, I put the butcher knife back in its box.

"You're an enlistee," I told her. "A comrade in arms. So I'd better treat you well. But listen, now that you're in my unit you'd better obey orders. In the army you have ranks and orders and that's it. I'm a veteran and you're just a new recruit, so you have to take care of me."

"You mean you want me to suck you, right?" Kirarin shouted disgustedly.

"That's right. So get to it—on the double."

I stomped over to her and grabbed her hair. "Knock it off!" she shouted, and easily brushed away my hand. Gooseflesh rippled up on my skin and I stood stock-still. I was remembering how it felt when I grabbed hold of my mom's hair and thought, She's a woman, but also how creepy my slutty old lady felt to me. What I mean is, I didn't just wipe out my mom's sins, but her sluttiness, too. So maybe her being slutty was part of what she was guilty of? The more I thought about it, the more I couldn't figure it out, and I gave the pillow that lay on the gray carpet a good kick.

"Why are you so obsessed with the army? Are you like one of those military nerds?"

Kirarin took a can of Pocari Sweat out of the fridge. I didn't tell her how I figured out that the soldier tortured by the Filipinos and I were one and the same. No sense in telling a slut such things. Kirarin sipped at her drink like it tasted really bad and said, "Why'd you kill your mom? And how'd you do it?"

I shrugged.

"Telling you isn't going to help any. Stop acting like a prosecutor."

"But I want to know," she insisted.

Kirarin swung her crossed legs. I was surprised to see that the downy hair on her legs was blond. The hair on my mom's legs was dark like a guy's. It always struck me as animal-like and grossed me out.

"Why's the hair on your legs like a foreigner's?"

"I bleach it," Kirarin said, making fun of me again, with this look on her face like, How in the world have you survived up till now without knowing that? "In the summer girls don't shave, they bleach it. While you guys are studying your butts off and jerking off, we girls are up to more clever things."

"Do that with mine, too."

"I didn't bring any bleach with me."

"Go buy some. There's gotta be a convenience store nearby."

Kirarin laughed her head off. "Now why would you want to do that? I thought you were on the run."

The answer was clear enough. I wanted to change into a different person, somebody much tougher. I thought it'd be cool to have blond leg hairs as my weapon, instead of the old salt suit. I got back in bed and lay down. I felt like I could still sleep forever. Kirarin inserted a couple of hundred-yen coins into the room TV. She flicked through a couple of news programs before finally settling on a music show. She turned around and said, "There's nothing on the news about you. The world's forgotten all about you."

I stood up.

"Really?"

"They were all so worked up about it, now there's nothing."

"Hey, who's the smartest of your friends?"

"Terauchi," she replied immediately. "She's got to be the bright-est. Her face is kind of classically pretty, and she's a little frumpy, but not too bad. But she's kind of dark sometimes, and you can't figure out what she's thinking. She's always fooling around saying dumb things, but when it's exam time she knows what she's doing and does a great job. She's kind of a mystery woman. No matter what, though, our group tends to rely on her. She can get on your nerves sometimes, and I can't stand it, but she can be a lot of fun, so I like her. Terauchi's dark side is kind of like yours. I'm not sure how, exactly. She might actually be nuts, just like you."

When I was calling all of the girls on Toshi's cell phone, Ter-auchi was the one who abruptly hung up on me. I found her reac-tion more soldierly than that of Yuzan or Kirarin. She's a real *cadet*. By cadet, I mean those elite officers who graduate from the mili-tary academy. The reason she says all kinds of stupid things is she's dumbing herself down to the level of girls like Kirarin and Yuzan. But when the pedal hits the metal, you could count on her to know what to do, 'cause she's a real soldier. All of sudden I thought maybe Terauchi was the only one who could help me out.

"Tell me more about her!"

"Hey, knock it off with that tone of voice, like you're ordering me around."

Kirarin stuck out her lips, her old flirty habits.

"Stop flirting," I said. "And sit up straight."

Kirarin frowned, clicked her tongue, and said something. I heard some voice mumbling this: "Duty is heavier than a moun-tain, death lighter than a feather."

"What was that you just said?" I asked. "You really know a lot more than I do."

"I didn't say anything."

Kirarin shot me a little disgusted look. So what was this—the hallucination hour? I was really happy. Who knows, maybe I *am* a genius after all. Problem is, nobody knows it. It's all my old lady's fault, her and her views on raising kids, and the kind of education she and my school forced down my throat. I should have told the world what a genius I am, but I blew it by not leaving any note behind in my room. Before I completely lost it, I should have written something down.

"They say juvenile offenders are most often precocious and extremely bright, people who can't adjust to the education system. So I think I should leave behind a novel or poem or something, like that murderer Sakakibara did, something to shake people up. Something to let people know how gifted I am."

"I don't know," Kirarin said. "Most of the time don't they just complain about their home life? How their parents mistreated them, or got divorced, how they weren't loved enough? But yours was a decent enough family."

"That's not what I'm talking about. I want to write a manifesto for my crime."

"So why don't you?"

Kirarin didn't seem to get it, and took another reluctant sip of her Pocari Sweat.

"I can't," I growled. "I don't have the time. They're chasing me. Plus, I have to get back to Tokyo to kill the old man. Who has the time?"

"So forget about it."

"I'm not going to forget about it. I want to get something down on paper before I kill my dad."

"Are you for real?" Kirarin shot me a serious look. "I say give it up. It'll just get the media all worked up again."

I ignored her. This was no time for logical arguments.

"I'll get Terauchi to write it. You said we're kind of alike, right?

She's smart and efficient. So I'll have Terauchi ghostwrite it for me. Make her part of my military staff. The head of propaganda."

"That's a dumb idea."

Kirarin dissolved in laughter, but I was deadly serious. I took the cell phone I'd re-requisitioned out of my pocket and handed it to her.

"Call Terauchi," I ordered her.

"Call her yourself."

"My battery's about out."

"Mine, too," she grumbled, but handed over her cell phone. "It's number five on the speed dial."

"What's up?" this listless girl's voice answered right away, like she'd been waiting for the call.

"It's me. Worm."

The line was silent for a second, and then she spoke briskly.

"You're kidding, right? Why the heck are you calling me? Don't bother me."

She spoke in this quick, low voice that revealed how smart she was. The kind of girl I have the most trouble dealing with. Totally different from a lowly foot soldier like Kirarin.

"I've got something to ask you," I said.

"It's so weird you'd use the nickname Worm yourself. It was Toshi who gave you that nickname."

"Whatever. That's not the point."

I was getting irritated, finding myself adjusting to her tempo.

"Is Kirarin really with you? Put her on."

While I was asleep Kirarin must have been phoning everyone. But I couldn't let on that I knew that.

"It's top secret, so I can't say."

"Don't worry about it," Terauchi said solemnly, "just put her on.

That's her phone you're using, right? So is she alive? At least tell me that."

There was no way around it, so I handed the phone to Kirarin. She answered in that cutesy, friendly voice she reserves for phone calls.

"Everything's fine, Terauchi. I'm so sorry I made you worry about me. I've been going through some really weird times, I can tell you that. I called my parents and told them I was staying over at your place, so play along, okay? I'll leave Worm after a while, so not to worry. He's not dangerous at all, though kind of weird. Just a sec, I'll put him back on. He said he wants your advice about something."

"My advice?!" Terauchi was pissed. "Listen, you're threatening Kirarin, right? She's a good kid, so don't trick her."

"You're the ones who've been tricked," I said. "You know something? She's pretty hot."

"What do you mean by that?"

Damn. I didn't give a shit about these girls' power relationships, their friendship, the kind of people they really were.

"Forget about it. I want you to ghostwrite something for me. How about it?"

"By ghostwrite do you mean a ghost story? Or maybe some horror story?" Terauchi said, trying to make a lame joke out of it.

"Gimme a break. I want you to pretend you're a boy who's killed his mother and write a story about it. It doesn't have to be long, but something that's better than what that killer Sakakibara wrote. Sprinkle in some Dostoyevsky or Nietzsche or whatever. But do a good job of incorporating those, so nobody can trace the source. Then sort of wrap it up like 'Evangelion.' Or maybe—it might be better to make it all avant garde–ish, know what I mean? Philosophy of life, moaning and groaning about the absurdity of it all, like that. I'm counting on you. If a story doesn't work out, then a poem's fine. If you make it kind of incomprehensible and look cool then a poem might just do the trick. The kind of poem that they could use as evidence in a psych evaluation, that sort of thing. Something that hides my real intentions and confuses the reader."

Terauchi's voice revealed her surprise.

"You want *me* to do this?" she asked. "Why me? You going to pay me? It's not worth it, even if you did. I mean, if they catch you then they'll print what I wrote. If people think it's well done, that doesn't do me any good. You'll get all the credit. If they don't like it and it comes out that I ghostwrote it, then *I'll* be in trouble. *Serious* trouble. So no matter how you cut it, it's a lose-lose situation for me."

"But if it doesn't come out that you wrote it and people think it stinks, then *I'm* the loser."

"Then why don't *you* write it?" Terauchi laughed through her nose.

"You idiot! If I could do that, I wouldn't have to ask for your help."

"You really can't write it, can you? What a joke. You're one of those kids at K High at the bottom of the barrel, right? You got in okay but burned out in the process. Well, forget it, I'm too busy. I'm taking three summer school classes—English, classical literature, and geography. Summer's a critical point for me, so why do I have to write your stupid manifesto? I have only five months left before entrance exams. They're gonna put you in juvie anyway, so what does it matter? Yuzan told me you're still saying stupid things like having to give up on taking the entrance exams for Tokyo University. You're just trying to show off. Loony guys like you who kill their mothers are the pits, you know that? You're still a child, but you're oblivious to that fact. Killing your mom, running from the law—what's the fun in that?"

"There's nothing fun about it."

"So why're you telling me to write a novel for you? You should write a memo yourself. That would be much more interesting, from a criminal psychology perspective."

Terauchi didn't sound like she was going to stop talking anytime soon. I wanted to tell her about how I transformed when I was riding around on that blazingly hot bike, but I didn't think it would make any difference. So I decided to go on the offensive.

"If you don't write it for me, you can kiss your friend good-bye. I just bought a butcher knife a while ago. Killing one person or two—it's all the same to me. I'll see what it feels like to stab somebody."

Killing one person or two—it's all the same to me. This clichéd phrase that killers use in movies wouldn't leave my mind. *Death is lighter than a feather.*

"Are you serious?"

Terauchi let out an unexpected shout. Behind me, Kirarin was saying, "He's lying! He's just trying to scare you!" I shoved her out of the way. She fell down behind me but was still laughing this weird kind of laugh, like the whole thing was hilarious. Going all hysterical on me. I covered the phone as best I could so Terauchi wouldn't hear. But Kirarin wouldn't stop laughing, so I covered her mouth with my hand.

"I might really kill her. My mind's already messed up. And if you tell the police about any of this, it's all over for her. Got it?"

"Yeah, I got it. I'll write it for you, don't worry." Terauchi sighed, giving in. "When do you want it by?"

"It's supposed to be something I wrote while I'm on the run, so try to do it quick. Within three days. If you can, e-mail it to

Kirarin's phone. I'll copy it down and carry it around with me. That way if they catch me, I can show it to them."

"So can I write it like a bunch of memos?"

"I told you already. Make it a story or a poem. Something creative."

"So it'd be cooler to have it not be something introspective?"

Terauchi was one smart girl, and I thought about what she said. Something introspective would negate my whole battle. I gave her a command: "Fight to the bitter end!"

"I got it. I'll be a regular kamikaze."

She said this very coolly and abruptly hung up. That click sounded to me like the limitless contempt she had for me. Made me angry. But I'd gotten one task squared away, which made me happy. I looked down at Kirarin, who was still on the floor. Her hysterics over, she was looking away from me sullenly.

"Lights out," I said. "Tomorrow we're going to rob a taxi to secure some funds."

I lay down on the bed but Kirarin stayed where she was, sprawled on the filthy carpet. It pissed me off, and I yelled at her.

"What's the matter? You planning to sleep there? What's your problem?"

"Nothing," she said, an upset girl's voice filtering up from the floor. But I was too starving to care. I'd had only a muffin in the morning and nothing since. No supply sergeant around. I shoved a pillow against my empty stomach and tried to get to sleep. Just then I heard sobbing coming from below.

"Stop crying. It bothers me."

"You mean you don't think of me as a woman?"

Maybe I *should* kill her. *Seriously.* I tried to control my anger as she went on with her rant.

"*I'm* the one who should be angry," she said. "I mean, what's the

point of me even being here? You've ripped my pride to shreds.
Nobody's ever treated me like this before. I knew you were weird,
but still I took a great risk in coming here to be with you. Spending
one night with a criminal, a guy who killed his mother—my repu-
tation's shot to hell. I'll never get married now. No more Cute
Kirarin—from now on it's *Dark* Kirarin. So how come you're acting so nice to Terauchi and letting her do this intellectual work
while all I am is a hostage? After you called me a new recruit and
were driving me so hard. It's not fair."

"She's a cadet, that's why."

"What do you mean, 'cadet'?"

"She's officer material."

All of a sudden, I sensed Kirarin standing up in the dark. It
actually scared me. I wanted to wipe out all the noisy women, all
the sluts in the world, but now I had one right in front of me who
was a total pain in the ass. I braced myself, thinking she was going
to try to mess up the secret agreement I'd gone to all that trouble
to make with Terauchi.

"Why the hell am I here, anyway?" Kirarin shouted. Her spit hit
my face, but I kept quiet. That's for you to figure out, I thought.
I'm busy with my own battles, and just surviving today is as much
as I can handle.

"Answer me. Why am I here?"

"You're the one who decided to come out here, not me."

"That's a lie," she said, sitting on the bed. "A lie! You're the one
who told me, 'I'll take you to another world.' That's why I came
here. Remember? You told me, 'Why don't we get transformed
together? I can make you into a new person. And we'll wipe the
smug smile off your ex-boyfriend's face.' You're playing around at
being a soldier, but you don't care about me at all. You've abandoned me. You asked Terauchi to write your poem or whatever for

you, but why not ask me? I can write a poem if I have to. Just throw some phrases together. *Anybody* can do that. Terauchi might be a cadet or whatever, but I'm a soldier, so you better not underestimate me. Or discriminate against me. You're so totally sneaky. If this is the kind of battle you're fighting, then count me out! It's just one awful thing after another."

I hadn't said these set phrases to Kirarin in order to recruit her into the army or anything. I'd just felt that way at the time. And now I just didn't feel like that at all. It's the truth, isn't it? Sure, it's a contradiction, but so what? I was tired and hungry, but still I tried to rack my poor brain to figure out how to quell this insurrection. Then all of a sudden she jumped on top of me and straddled me. She was heavy and I let out a gasp.

"Get off me, stupid."

Kirarin pinned my two arms above my head and whispered in my ear.

"Or maybe I should take *you* to another world? You act all cool, but you're just a virgin. Why don't you come back in ten years."

A slut. A real slut. Kirarin's thin hip joints rubbed against my belly and even though I was pissed, I got hard right away. I had no clue what to do. Nobody's ever told me how to do it with a woman. I mean, I wasn't dealing here with some cute "li'l sis" who'd take her pants off at my command. Girls were guys' playthings only in manga. I shoved away her arms and drew her close. Her soft body felt great. Her slim frame, her hair with a slight scent of sweat. So I was finally going to get laid. Maybe it'd be like in Mishima's story "Patriotism," all hot and heavy. I pictured that photo of Mishima, dressed only in a loincloth, brandishing a Japanese sword, and suddenly I froze. Wasn't I supposed to be beyond needing a girl? How could I get the spirit and the flesh to work together here? I was off my guard, and Kirarin sent me flying and I banged my head on the headboard.

"Ow! What are you doing?"

"You're pathetic. A soldier who's terrible at sex is terrible in war, too."

Damn. I grabbed her tight. I had to get on top, rip her clothes off, spread her legs, and put it inside. But how? If I ordered her to suck me, would she really put my cock in her mouth without a fight? Was this like a wartime rape or something? Ideas were spinning around in my brain, but none of the simulations I came up with were of any help. What a pain. Maybe I *should* go ahead and waste her. My brain was short-circuiting and all I could come up with was this simple solution. I was impatient. This was war. *War. Kill her!* In the gloom, I could tell that Kirarin was staring at me. Then she spoke in this cold-as-ice voice.

"Knock it off. Don't touch me. I don't feel like sleeping with a murderer."

I let her go. I was afraid of this real enemy now, of Kirarin. The enemies I should be battling—the police, society—still hadn't shown up. But right in front of me was another kind of enemy. A wall I couldn't climb over. Kill! *Kill!!* Shut off the brain circuits.

"I was just too caught up in this whole thing about getting revenge on Wataru," Kirarin was saying. "When you told me you'd show me another world, it got me all excited. But being with you isn't going to lead to anything good. I can tell that now."

She got out of bed and ran her fingers through her hair.

"I'm not interested in you anymore," she said. "I'm going home."

Was she serious? I was suddenly pulled back to reality.

"Give me the money for the room," I said.

"No way. That'd make me an accomplice."

My brain circuits went *poof!* and shorted out again. Smoke coming out and everything. I jumped into action. I grabbed the box in my backpack, the one with the butcher knife. When Kirarin saw this, she gave a little scream.

"Get down on your knees," I commanded.

Kirarin knelt down on the floor and bowed in front of me. I stepped on her long hair. I could feel her shaking through my leg. That's right—that's how you surrender.

"I'm sorry," she said. "*Really.* If you need money, I'll give it to you."

"I'll requisition the money. You stay here. That's an order."

I stayed awake, keeping watch over the POW to make sure she didn't escape. The prisoner was sobbing, but then she fell asleep. I occupied the sofa and went through her belongings that I'd confiscated. A purse with 18,600 yen. A student ID card. Her swollen purse was filled with cards from various stores, a library card, a commuter pass, and so on. I looked at the photo of her on the ID. In her school uniform she looked even more like a "li'l sis." Long hair, slightly droopy eyes, and a perplexed look. Her lips pouty, pretending to be sweet and innocent. The exact kind of girl the perverts in my class would drool over. A small makeup bag was stuffed full of things—a handkerchief, tissue paper, lipstick, deodorant, oil-blotting tissue. Her cell phone. In the bottom of her bag was a movie theater ticket stub. It was just three days ago I was enjoying talking with the prisoner about movies. Seemed more like thirty years ago.

I was terribly lonely then, heading for the swimming pool my family used to go to, and I was upset, wondering if there was some way of reversing time. So the prisoner's sweet voice made me happy at the moment. But not now—it just pisses me off like you wouldn't believe. Not just the prisoner, but *all* of them piss me off—my old man, relatives, our house. You name it. Everything and everybody just got in the way now, and all I wanted was to go somewhere, *anywhere,* as long as it was far away from them.

I was getting closer to the real essence of who I am. A revelation was welling up from inside me. What that essence was, I had no idea, but I was getting more and more confused, my existence more pointless by the minute. Is that who I am? Is that all? I got awfully sad, and tears started to stream down my face. I wiped away my tears with the prisoner's handkerchief, which smelled like perfume and detergent. From out of nowhere I felt like reality was going to crush me. The reality of having murdered my mother. Fight on! Fight on! I tried like crazy to stifle the tears. Just then the prisoner's cell phone rang. It was Toshi. I felt rescued.

"Hi," she said. "Sorry for calling back so late. I didn't realize I had a message."

"It's me," I said.

"Oh, I see. What about Kirarin?" Toshi wasn't surprised at all. "Is she there?"

"She's asleep."

"Are you doing okay? Are you all right?" I didn't know what to say. "It's one o'clock already. Why aren't you asleep? Can't you sleep?"

I hate kind girls. They're dangerous. A warning buzzer went off inside me. *Danger! Danger!* I had no clue why.

"Hey, did you hear me?"

"I'm listening," I said.

"Yuzan said Kirarin got in touch with her. When she said she was with you, I couldn't believe it. I guess I never thought she was interested in you."

I'm not interested in you anymore. The prisoner's comment came back to me.

"Your dad stopped by our house today."

"How come?"

"Just to apologize for all the trouble. Seems like he's making the rounds of the neighbors. He said he can't sleep at night, wondering where his son is, wandering somewhere. He's miserable about losing his wife, but he said that all he can think of is saving his son's soul. At night when he's all alone in the house, he obsesses over what happened and blames himself. He said sometimes he wants to die. And when he feels like that, he says he keeps himself together by staring at straight lines for all he's worth."

"Straight lines?" I said in a loud voice. "What do you mean?"

"Objects that are straight. Like the frame of a shoji screen or a pillar. Staring at things that are straight, he said, makes him feel like there's a world that's still stable and solid. He said he can be more objective that way. He can objectively keep his act together and wait for his son to come home."

What a load of crap. My old man was so full of it, I didn't know what to say. A stable world this late in the game? The world had come undone and floated away long ago. The idiot. *Objective*—what sort of crap is that? That's why all you can see is a totally flat world. I made up my mind right then and there—I might be confused, but I was going to forge ahead. Toward the even more incomprehensible, chaotic front lines. Confusion. If the old man looked at straight lines to keep his act together, I was going to stare at *curved* lines and go down in flames. My eyes flitted around the room, looking for curved lines. Wall, floor, ceiling, door, TV. Straight lines everywhere.

Then I looked over at the body of my prisoner, lying in the bed.

"Hey, Worm," Toshi said. "Can you hear me?"

I switched off the cell phone.

There really are things that are irreparable. I'm always wanting to tell people this. It doesn't matter who I say it to. It could be a rainy day and I'm standing on the station platform of the Keiō Line, waiting for an express train that's late. Or I'm standing in line at a convenience store where a brand-new employee is slowly working the register. Either way, I see myself muttering this without thinking. Like the phrase has wormed its way into my unconscious so much that, when I'm irritated, I can't help but blurt it out.

I don't think I could blurt it out to Yuzan or Kirarin, though. They'd just say, "Hmm. You could be right," their eyes dreamily looking around for a bit, but then, as soon as the subject changed, they'd forget all about it. They'd drop it so fast I'd be left there feeling stupid and embarrassed. I'd hate that, so that's why I don't bring it up with them. It'd be like a lighthouse, where the spotlight rotates and, for an instant, illuminates something. But once the light moves on, everything melts back into the dark. They couldn't care less. Unless you actually experience something that can't be undone, you can't possibly understand it. People like that just think it's some phrase and misinterpret it. To them, it's some cheap truism.

Toshi alone might react differently. On the surface she acts all casual, but she's a sensitive person and is very intuitive. I bet she'd look me in the eye and try to tease out what I'm getting at. But not finding anything, Toshi, too, would soon be disappointed and turn to other things.

By "things that are irreparable," I don't mean something

like Worm's killing his mother. It's not that simple. And it's not something like the guilt Yuzan has over avoiding her mother's death. It's actually the opposite. How can I put it? Once you're dead you can't come back to life—it's final. But to my way of thinking, those are also events that aren't entirely irreparable, because they are the easy way out. I mean, death is something everybody's going to experience someday, so it's an easy-to-understand ending Worm's chosen, and in that sense something close to defeat. Killing somebody is just payback motivated by all your anger, humiliation, and desires, and since it doesn't put an end to problems, it doesn't fit in the category of an irreparable action. Something that's really irreparable is more like this: a horribly frightening feeling that keeps building up inside you forever until your heart is devoured. People who carry around the burden of something that can't be undone will one day be destroyed.

Are my ideas too complicated? I'm the kind of person who thinks about difficult things more than others. That's why at home and at school I'm always joking around. The reason's simple—even if I exposed the real me to other people, they wouldn't understand. Toshi might pick up a little of what's going on, but I've yet to meet a person—child or adult—who really *gets* me.

There's this huge gap between me and other people—a gap in ability, experience, and feelings. I'm really emotional, and bright. When I say bright I don't mean good at schoolwork. I mean I can think abstractly. Some adults might think a high school student can't do this, but they're wrong.

I feel above human relationships, so I'm constantly holding myself in check. Controlling myself like this zaps all my energy, so I gave up on studying and don't take it seriously. I figured out long ago that studying for exams is nothing more than figuring out how to work the system.

When I became a senior in high school, we all took this psychological test. It was a multiple-choice test with two hundred totally stupid questions on it and you had to choose things like "I tend to go along with what other people are saying." I decided to see how far I could fool people, so I deliberately made a total mess of it. Toshi, Yuzan, and Kirarin—all the bright ones in our class—did the same thing, but the only one called into the guidance counselor's cubbyhole office afterward was me. Seems my homeroom teacher had quietly put in a call to my parents.

So I went, partly curious, partly disgusted, and as you can imagine this middle-aged woman in a navy blue suit, no makeup, was waiting for me. She told me her name—Suzuki or Sato, some totally banal name—and I forgot it right away.

"You would be Kazuko Terauchi? I'd like to meet with you a few times to talk over things."

"What kind of things?" I asked.

"What you think about, and any worries you might have."

What good's going come from talking with the likes of you? Why do I have to do this? Trying to hold back my rising anger, I gave my usual silly laugh. My weapon is that I can hide my feelings and say something stupid to cover them up. Toshi's weapon is her made-up name, Ninna Hori. For Kirarin, it's always pretending to be cheerful. Yuzan's the only one who painfully exposes herself to the world.

"I don't have any worries," I said. "Other than college entrance exams."

Entrance exams, the woman noted down on a sheet of white paper. I sneered inside. We met like that a total of three times. I made up a story about being afraid my friends might exclude me from their group and this seemed to satisfy her and no more summonses came to meet with her.

Each time I met her I became more and more frightened of adults. She just listened silently to my made-up stories, smiling. I was frightened by the optimism of adults, their stupid trust in science to treat a troubled heart. Afraid of their obsession with believing they *have* to treat troubled kids. I just wanted them to leave me alone, so how come they didn't get it? But that's the way it always is.

I've got to hand it to them, though—adults, that is. They've created this society where lies are uncovered. The woman told me proudly that these psych tests were able to ferret out any untruths you would tell. It turned out I'd scored the highest of anyone on the test. Higher than anyone in any other school or even school district. Which meant that they saw right through me, that I'm a person who wants to hide a lot of stuff. That much they definitely found out. But I don't think they could pinpoint what it is I want to hide. There's no way I want to get some treatment from the school, or a middle-aged guidance counselor with her know-it-all face. I mean, over these last five years, the only one who's been thinking about all this is me. And the only one who really understands me is *me*.

Like I did with the counselor, I always say stupid things in order to be vague and evasive. Toshi, though, sees right through my attempt to dodge other people and it seems to bother her. One time, I can't remember exactly when, she and I were talking about the future, something we hardly ever do, and all of a sudden she totally lost it.

"You're laughing but your eyes aren't," she said.

I put a happy look on my face and pretended to smile. I had a bunch of dumb gags I knew how to use. All of which disgusted people.

"I am too laughing!" I said.

"That's a lie. You can't fool me, joking around all the time."

"Dude. That's just me. I'm gonna grab me one of those Tokyo or Hitotsubashi University guys, get married, and be a full-time housewife."

"How can you give up like that?"

Toshi could always guess exactly what I was feeling. I tried whispering in her ear: *Romance!* But after staring back at me, she said, like there were no two ways about it, "Terauchi, you're a total mystery."

"Why do you say that?"

"Knock it off, okay? I know for a fact that you're hiding something. *Everybody* knows it."

"I'm not hiding anything. Dude—it's true."

"Forget it," Toshi said, looking hurt.

Toshi had just been telling me about her typical high school woes—how even if she went to college, she had no idea what she wanted to be. She added that this was something she hardly ever told people. And she was pissed because I didn't show any interest and basically made no effort to take her seriously. Then, abruptly, she looked at me with this worried expression.

"Tell me," she said, "did you have some awful experience in your past?"

"No, nothing."

Think some seventeen-year-old kid's gonna trap me like that? No way. Of course, I'd just barely turned eighteen myself, but I really had no sense of how old I was. Was I a child, an adult, or a senior citizen? Toshi is smart and kind, and growing up with nice parents like that there's no way she'd end up as complicated as me. You want to try to be like me? Be my guest. It's funny how sometimes I act like an ordinary high school girl, eating lunch with the girls—Toshi, Yuzan, Kirarin—going out to karaoke clubs with them. But this is me faking it, trying to show people I'm just having a trouble-free high school life like any other girl.

The truth is, I'm a disagreeable person who's always observing my friends with a cool, detached eye. So no wonder Toshi's pissed at me. I'm this sort of contrary person who thinks the only people worth knowing are those who get angry with me, but when they do get angry, I cleverly hide myself.

Yuzan pretends to be complicated like me, but she's really pretty simple. Right now, she's basically troubled over how to accept herself, whoever she is. Once she accepts that she's a lesbian, then she should be able to live that sort of life peacefully. With Kirarin, I think someday a guy will change her. So in that sense the two of them are basically wholesome. Which is a good thing, don't get me wrong. I'm not being sarcastic or anything. I really feel that way.

"I want you to pretend you're a boy who's killed his mother and write a story about it."

This is what Worm said to me on the phone. Naturally there's no way I'm going to do what he asked. I have no idea what kind of person he is, and if it's true that he murdered his mother, his mind has definitely reverted to the infantile. According to my theory, he's chosen a life that's the exact opposite of mine, since he avoided doing something irreparable and instead did something lazy. No need to waste my precious time creating something for a guy like that. The other three can baby him if they want. Someday there'll be a day of judgment.

I can't figure out why Yuzan and Kirarin would be interested in a guy like that. I'd like to see them nail Worm soon, haul him before a counselor like that middle-aged lady or a psychiatrist or somebody, and bombard him with questions day after day. Let him put himself into the hands of modern science, with its ideology that people can be saved, and see how his way of thinking fares then. Then he'll see how twisted and petty he's been.

What I find most interesting is how each of our personalities is reflected in how we've reacted to this whole affair. Toshi is kind, so she feels bad for Worm's murdered mother and worries about what the future might hold for him. Yuzan's projected herself onto Worm and helped him escape. And Kirarin, who's taken off with him, has this whole illusory image of him and hopes she'll be changed by being with him. Everybody knows that she hooks up with guys in Shibuya and was jilted by one guy in particular, but she acts like it's some big secret.

My theory is that Yuzan and Kirarin are using Worm's crime to look down on him. Toshi's reaction is more what you'd expect, the standard attitude of your typical bystander. And me—well, I plan to confront Worm head-on and tell him where he's wrong. Not about his killing his mother. What I want to criticize is, as I've said many times, his naiveté in thinking his actions are irreparable.

The door of my room suddenly swung open without a knock. Same as always, so I wasn't surprised. It was my kid brother, Yukinari.

"Have you been online?" he asked. "They posted a photo of the guy." Yukinari's voice, which hadn't changed yet, was raspy and sexless.

"What guy?"

"The kid from K High who killed his mother."

I'd been lying on the bed but got up and went next door to his

room. Yukinari was a freshman in an elite private junior high he'd
just entered this spring. During the five years he's attended cram
school it's like his personality's changed. He's become much more
clever than me, more cunning. You'd never catch Yukinari doing
something irreparable—he's too smart to ruin his life like that.

The computer he got as a present for getting into junior high
was plunked down in the middle of his desk, its LCD screen
reflecting the pale fluorescent lights on the ceiling. On the screen
was a photo of Worm wearing his school uniform. It was kind of
grainy, like it was blown up from a school group photo. But his
special look was clear enough. The small head jutting out of the
uniform collar, the narrow eyes. He held his chin up high, so his
neck looked long, and he had an arrogant expression. His eyebrows were set apart, the corners of his eyes turned up. He looked
like those Japanese men from a long time ago, the kind you see in
photo collections from the Meiji period.

"So Worm has this classical sort of face," I said.

"Looks kind of like Shinsaku Takasugi, the Meiji Restoration
leader." After he said this, Yukinari, sitting at his desk, looked at
me suspiciously. "The guy's called Worm? How'd you know that?"

"Toshi told me."

"It's perfect. They said he goes to K High. A K High student
who killed his mother—that's enough to make him a hero. He
looks pretty full of himself. Imagine a senior getting worked up
enough to kill his mother." Yukinari's tone was sarcastic as he
scrolled down the Web site with ease. The school that Yukinari
attended was a private school one rank down from K High.

"He's a hero because he's in K High?"

Yukinari spit out his reply: " 'Cause he's an elite kid who fell."

On the Web site bulletin board was a conversation thread titled
"Support for A, the boy who killed his mother." There were a ton

of half-baked posts purporting to be sightings: "I saw him riding his bike down Highway 18." "There was a guy that looks like him reading porno magazines in a convenience store in Kochi." "I saw him in a public bath washing his back." "He was at Disneyland dressed up as Goofy." Plus some irresponsible posts in support of him, saying things like "Hope you can elude them. I'm with you." I realized that these supporters had ideas exactly like Yuzan's: self-centered sentiments, easygoing sympathy.

Still, I couldn't figure out why all these people were rooting for him.

"Maybe they're supporting him 'cause he's trying to escape on a bicycle?" I asked.

"Guess so. He's kind of childish, though."

Yukinari quickly slid his mouse down, scrolling farther down the page. At the very end was this: "Question. Why didn't you kill your father while you were at it? Heh, heh, heh." Right below this was a reply from somebody pretending to be A, the boy involved. "There's already someone who killed both his parents with a bat. Pride in being from K High won't allow me to do a copycat murder." Yukinari pointed to the question part. "I wrote this one," he said.

"You mean you want to kill Dad?"

"Don't be illogical," Yukinari said, annoyed.

We could hear the front door open, and it sounded like Dad had come home. He didn't say, "I'm home," or anything, but cleared his throat, so we knew it was him. He puttered around noisily, switching on the AC in the living room, taking a bath, opening the fridge door. Dad works at a metropolitan bank and leaves early in the morning and comes home late every night. Nobody was paying him any attention.

"Good timing," I said. "Dad's back."

"What the hell for? Too bad he wasn't run over. Maybe if we're lucky he'll be hit by a taxi," Yukinari muttered. I imagined this was how he spent every night, surfing the Web, muttering expletives.

"I wonder if the cops are checking out this Web site."

"Of course they are," Yukinari answered coldly, and was printing out the photo of Worm. "You can have this, sis. Put it up in your room."

"Why?"

"A nice memento. Or you can give it to Toshi."

This startled me. Yukinari had no idea that the four of us were in contact with Worm. The photo most definitely would be a souvenir of our involvement in this whole affair. And a memento revealing the essence of who we really were. If Worm got caught, the photos posted online would be of the four of *us*, with some caption like, "The four high school girls who aided and abetted." Kirarin would no doubt be the most popular. I took the photo of Worm out of the printer and went back to my room. Right then my cell phone rang.

"It's me. So how're you doing with it?"

It was Worm. No "Hi, can you talk now?" or anything. The guy wouldn't know good manners if they bit him on the leg. I switched over to my control-the-temper mode. His last call was last night. Which means they haven't caught him yet, I thought, as I gazed at the photo of him, at his scrawny neck.

"What'd ya mean, 'it'?"

"My criminal manifesto." Worm must have been outside, because every once in a while I heard cars driving by.

"Didn't you say you wanted it to be a novel?" I asked.

"It doesn't matter. A poem's fine. Some cool lines, like from a play. I'm counting on you."

Since he's having somebody else write it, you know that in the end if he doesn't like it he's going to change parts, or maybe toss the whole thing anyway.

"Why not just take something from a manga?" I asked coldly.

"It's gotta be original. I'm a high school student, for God's sake! Can't wind up losing out to some fourteen-year-old kid."

"Then I think you'd better give up the whole idea. You've already totally lost out."

"You're a real slut, you know that?" Worm sounded more relaxed than the night before. "You're getting to be just like my old lady."

I decided then and there I was never going to have any kids. The last thing I want is to give birth to some idiot like him.

I pretended to be hurt. "Don't say things like that."

"Sorry . . ."

"Okay then. I'll start writing the thing," I said, lying through my teeth, but trying to sound meek and obedient.

"Then get going. Have to get it done before I can go kill my father."

I didn't go there; instead I asked him where he was.

"Karuizawa," Worm answered, not wary at all. "It's nice and cool here. We broke into a vacant summer cottage. Taking a break. Tomorrow we move out to the front lines."

"Is Kirarin with you?"

"Hello? Terauchi? It's me, Kirarin."

Instead of Worm answering, Kirarin came on the line all of a sudden but soon stopped talking. "Go away," I heard her say, and then Worm complained, "I'm not listening."

"Dude. Sounds like you and the murderer are getting along just fine," I told her.

"Stop it. Nothing's happening. I'm with him 'cause he threatened me."

For somebody being threatened, she sounded pretty cheerful.

"I hear you're in Karuizawa."

"That's right. We just got back from eating ramen. Mount Asama looks totally weird at night," she said tranquilly. "I'm going back to Tokyo tomorrow, so don't worry about me. But there's something I wanted to ask you, Terauchi. I don't see anything about Worm in the papers or on TV. Do you have any idea of how the murder's being reported?"

"There doesn't seem to be anything in the media about it. His picture's online, though. On the Internet people seem to really be into it."

With my toe I played with the photo of Worm. So Kirarin was doing it with a guy who looked like Shinsaku Takasugi, I thought, strangely moved.

"You're kidding," she said. "What should we do? They know what he looks like."

Kirarin let out this exaggerated sigh. She was taking Worm's side now, I noticed. Worm came back on the line.

"Is my photo really online? Gotta be those jerks at school. What a crappy thing to do. Course, if I was in their shoes I'd probably do the same. I knew it was going to happen sometime, but didn't figure it'd be this soon. But I've got a girl with me, so they won't recognize me."

When he said this, it struck me that Kirarin wasn't coming home as easily as she thought. Worm found it convenient to have Kirarin with him, and he was too sly to let her go. Kirarin was a cute girl whom everybody liked, so maybe I shouldn't have let on about his photo being on the Internet. But being with Worm was something Kirarin had decided on her own. A Kirarin who was totally different from me.

"So you're serious about wanting a manifesto?" I asked.

"Yep. Any good ideas?"

"How about this? 'Why didn't you kill your father while you were at it? Heh, heh, heh.'" What my brother had written online.

Worm reacted immediately. "That's just not me. Writing someone else's impressions is not going to get us anywhere. 'Death is lighter than a feather, and I'm resigned to it.' Now *that's* pretty cool."

"The Imperial Rescript for Soldiers and Sailors. Fits you to a T."

"Guess so," Worm replied, giving my indifferent response a bit of thought. Then, as if he'd roused himself, he said, "Okay, now that I have a slogan, maybe I should go and kill the old man?"

What're you talking about, slogans? This isn't China, pal. And I had my doubts about whether such crummy words would do. Worm didn't understand the concept of something that can't be undone, after all. At this point, Worm meant nothing to me. Less than a foreign body or a speck of poison.

"Don't ask me. How should I know? Hey, where exactly are you in Karuizawa?"

"We just left a ramen place along Highway Eighteen. We're gonna stop by a convenience store and then go back."

"Yeah? Well, take care then."

I said this without meaning it and hung up. I immediately dialed Toshi to give her an update. I'd already told her about last night and was sure she wanted to catch up on everything.

"So Kirarin's planning to stay with him?" Toshi said. "This is the worst possible scenario."

"I suppose so, but you have to remember that's what she chose to do."

"Terauchi, you really are cold, you know that?" Toshi said in her usual tone.

"Can't help it. Kirarin's seventeen and an adult."

"I know, but what're we going to do?"

"When they arrest him, they'll check his cell phone records and then we'll be in deep trouble. Man—how could this happen?"

"I know," Toshi agreed. "I never imagined I'd get involved. An accomplice to murder—and aiding and abetting a fugitive. Or maybe just the aiding and abetting part? This is all because Yuzan helped him out."

"But didn't it start out by you lying?"

Toshi clammed up. Finally she let out a painful breath.

"I guess so," she said. "I felt sorry for the guy. I didn't want to help him, but I also didn't want him to get caught. So I just let things run their course, which means, yeah, I'm pretty responsible here."

"I think that he *wanted* us to get involved," I said, voicing a doubt I'd been having for a long time. "I mean, it was strange from the beginning that he'd phone all of us like that using your cell phone."

"But why would he want to do that?"

"You got me." But I felt I could understand what Worm was feeling. Loneliness. Sometimes that awful feeling causes you to do something stupid.

"You know," Toshi said, "I still can't fathom what Yuzan did. Why she had to leap into it like that. And speaking of Yuzan, I haven't heard from her. Has she called you?"

I could pretty much guess why there'd been no word from her. She realized that Worm didn't like a mannish girl like her, so she didn't feel like helping him run away anymore.

Right after I talked to Toshi I could faintly hear a car pull up into our apartment's parking lot. I'd closed the window because of the AC but now I opened it and looked down to the street level, seven floors below. Over in the corner of the lot was a four-wheel-drive vehicle backing into a spot. Not Mom's car. She wouldn't be back this early. I lay back down on the bed and gazed at the photo of Worm. It was too stressful, so I tossed it underneath the bed, where it stirred up the dust. I was in a self-induced depression. Welcome to my Real World.

I've taken the train to school ever since elementary school. My parents wanted me to go to a private elementary school in the city. It takes thirty-five minutes from P Station in Fuchu City, the Tokyo suburb where we live, to S Station in Shibuya Ward. Since the train goes all the way into the center of Tokyo, it's always packed.

I think it's cruel to make a little elementary school girl ride the train like that every day to school. P Station is in the suburbs, so the train isn't crowded when I get on. It's not like I can always get a seat, but there are usually very few people standing and you can relax. Mom told me when she saw how uncrowded the train was she felt confident I could commute by myself. At first Dad said it's okay, he'd go with me, but after a while he was transferred to some other city where he had to live by himself. So I was left alone. Dad came back to live with us when I was in fourth grade, but he didn't work in a downtown office anymore.

I'd squeeze myself into a space next to the door and stand there. With each station the number of passengers increased and I'd start to get squashed. One time I was pushed from behind, fell forward, and cut my cheek on the metal clasp of a woman's handbag. Another time my backpack hit an office worker who was sitting at the end of the row of seats and she shoved me away. After that I stopped standing next to the door.

Countless times I tried to get off at S station, where my school was, only to find myself stuck between people, unable to shake my backpack loose, so I'd have to get off at the next station. One time I felt faint, leaned against some old guys, and wound up going all the way to Shinjuku. But never once did any adult try to help me.

"Why is an elementary school kid riding such a packed train anyway?" this middle-aged office worker once complained to the guy sitting next to him when my backpack was poking him in the side and he had to twist away. I looked up then, trying to gauge the reaction of the other passengers. The middle-aged guy he'd spoken to just smiled sympathetically at what the other guy had said.

"Poor kid. Elementary school children should go to their local school."

"Little girl, you have it tough every day, don't you? Aren't you worn out?" the first middle-aged guy said, giving me a hard time. "Were you the one who said you wanted to go to a private school? I really doubt it."

"Have you told your mother how tough it is for you riding the trains? How you're causing trouble for other passengers?" said the guy next to him.

They were blaming my parents, not me, but I was the real object of their criticism, the weakest link, a tiny girl lugging a heavy backpack on a packed train. This was like heaven's punishment on my parents for choosing this cruel commute for me. A punishment which consisted of the unfair maliciousness, the truly awful way I was treated. This was my reality.

One morning I'd caught a cold and wasn't feeling well. It was pouring outside so the windows were shut tight, clouding up with all the CO_2 the passengers were breathing out. I started to feel really bad, suddenly couldn't stand it anymore, and threw up my breakfast on the lap of a person seated in front of me. It was a nicely dressed young woman, an office worker by the look of her, and when she saw this mess—the half-digested toast and stinky yogurt—all over her blue skirt, she was close to tears.

"Damn! Why'd you do that? I'm going to work now and what am I supposed to do?"

There wasn't much she could do. With tears in her eyes, she did her best to wipe herself off with a tissue. The other passengers didn't say a word, putting up with the stink of my vomit, trying their best to edge away whenever I frowned and they thought I might hurl again. No one tried to console me or comfort me. After that, I avoided standing in front of the seats, too.

When I got into the upper grades in elementary school, I got physically stronger and no longer threw up or had trouble getting off at the right station. But worse things began to happen. Perverts would surround me on the train. It was always the same men. I knew what these guys looked like, so I tried all sorts of things to avoid them—taking a different car, changing the time I left for school or home. But even if I could avoid this group of perverts there were always new ones, no matter which train I rode.

A few men would surround me and when I couldn't escape, they would feel me up. One liked to stroke my bare thighs. Another stroked my butt. And another would press my breasts, which were just beginning to show. If I yelled, they'd quickly turn away, transformed in an instant into ordinary office workers and students. But then after a while they'd be back at it. I was easy prey for perverts. I was young, weaker than them, and an obvious target. I couldn't stand it. Even though I was only in grade school, it taught me a painful lesson—that adult men are dirty and my enemies. I complained to my parents, telling them I didn't want to go to school anymore, didn't want to ride the train. But I never told them the real reason. I worried about them finding out that they'd put me in a situation where I had to suffer like this. As I continued to commute, before I knew it I was acting more adult than my own parents.

One day when I felt the perverts start to approach, I laughed out loud, this foolish laugh. And guess what? The pervs looked startled and scared. When I laughed at each one, he'd give me this revolted look and edge away. I'd finally discovered a method to drive them away: by changing something inside me, exchanging it for something else, and acting like an idiot. This is what I mean by something *irreparable*.

Actually there're other irreparable things, too. One of them started when my mother was having an affair. I guess it's more accurate to say she fell in love, rather than just had an affair. If I brought it up with Kirarin, she'd probably say something like "Nothing unusual about that. Happens all the time" and give examples of other people who were having affairs. Toshi would sympathize with my mom and say, "Even mothers fall in love at least once." Only fastidious Yuzan would look down at her feet, not trying to find the right words to say.

If Worm found out that his mother was having an affair, maybe he'd still hate her, but I wonder if he might not have killed her. Even though this is the road to something that can't be undone.

I could live with the fact that Mom was having an affair. Not for Kirarin's reasons—that it's a commonplace event, nothing to worry about. Or for Toshi's—that everyone should be free to fall in love. I didn't accept it because of any reasonable arguments like these; rather, I could forgive the unforgivable because I loved my mom more than anybody else, so I accepted what she was doing. I submitted to her, in other words—kind of like the way I accepted riding the train to school every day. When you don't have the strength to fight against fate, you just have to accept what comes. That's something that can't be undone.

When my kid brother started elementary school, my mother, who'd left her job for years to raise her children, decided to go back to work. I was in sixth grade at the time. My mother worked as a freelance producer. At the time I didn't know what this sort of work involved, that's just what it said on her business card. It isn't like a movie or TV producer, Mom explained to me—what she did was create business plans, helping to bring people together. I'd always had this one image of my mother and I remember what a shock it was when I saw this totally different side of her. For thirty-eight, she was still young and beautiful. She was a forceful person, overflowing with energy; since she never hesitated to argue with Dad, it's no exaggeration to say that in our family she was the one in charge. At the same time, I wasn't yet the "complicated" person I later became.

Mom stayed away from work for so long because Dad didn't want her to go back until my kid brother started elementary school. When my kid brother began attending the local public school, I remember the argument Mom and Dad had on the first day of classes. Mom wanted to put my brother into an after-school program, but Dad felt sorry for him and said he was too young. I was listening in the next room, thinking, Hey, if you feel sorry for him, think about *me*, riding the packed train to school every day! But Dad was confident he was doing the right thing, sending me to this expensive private school because I could get a better education there. Even if I told him what it was really like for me, I doubt his confidence would have wavered.

I should state up front that this is all just conjecture. I really don't know exactly what my parents thought about my commuting and my kid brother's after-school activities. But I think my father, who worked at a bank, was the kind of person who had a deep-seated prejudice against nursery schools and after-school programs and the like, and secretly felt that children whose mothers worked never amounted to anything. Ever since I was little, Mom fought Dad over this and gave in to him.

In the end, they wound up sending my brother to abacus class, a swim club, and various other lessons to fill up his time after school. From second grade on, they sent him to an after-hours cram school, thinking it was more efficient to consolidate it all in one school. Since then, his life has been filled with lessons and studying. The poor kid, some people might say. Others might think he's a victim of adults' lives. But that was our family's new lifestyle.

But I don't feel that it's anybody's fault that my brother and I led this kind of forced life. I can understand my parents' desire for us to get a better education, and I can really understand my mom's wanting to go back to work. I can even, to a degree, understand my dad insisting that kids need their mothers at home. Everyone insisted on getting what they wanted—that was the only way. And this new life of ours, where everyone sort of compromised on their desires, began when my kid brother started elementary school.

I'm not sure when my mother, now out working, began to change. Maybe in the early spring, just after I finished my second year in junior high. All of a sudden she stopped coming home at night on the weekends (as a freelancer, she often worked on odd days). When I asked her about it, she said that they were busy at work and often had to pull all-nighters. Did any of us work up the nerve to go to her office to check out her story? No way.

I started to feel anxious about the way Mom began to speak and act, the way she just sort of stared off into space half the time. I sensed that when she was home, her mind was on some destination far away from us, and it started to scare us. The reason being that, like I said, Mom ruled at home. Perhaps our life had changed because of *her* desires, not Dad's. Plus, there was the fact that Mom had way more charm and personality than Dad.

Every time Mom went on a trip I was afraid she'd never come back and I had terrible nightmares. I can still remember one in which she was dead. Dead, but still talking to me, repeating this one line over and over: "I've got to go." I thought I'd never see her again, which made me so sad I couldn't stand it, and in the dream I tried to stop her, and was crying. I still needed her.

My mom always came back from her trips, but she seemed sad and didn't look like herself. I sensed something was going on with her, but didn't have the courage to ask her directly. When I saw her and Dad going at it, I imagined she was sad because she wanted a divorce, but I couldn't figure out why she wanted to leave him so much. He was stubborn, to be sure, but other than that was a pretty decent person. Adults did such stupid things, yet they remained a mystery, making me suffer. That's when I decided I had to do some investigating if I wanted to really know what was going on.

One day, in my second year of high school, I stole her cell phone from her handbag while she was asleep. There were tons of e-mails from this one guy.

> Sorry I couldn't call you today. I was so busy at work I couldn't find a moment to call. Next time we meet I have lots to talk about. All I think about is you. Good night. Love you!

I've been thinking about you, and about what you
said. The two of us are like air plants. Our roots don't
grow in the soil. Which makes me wonder what's
keeping us together. Can love alone nourish a life? I
don't know. I love you.

So Mom was in love with some unknown man. Finally it
dawned on me that she'd totally abandoned us all—Dad, me, and
my kid brother. She was no longer the mother I used to know. I
struggled like crazy to find traces of the former phantom mother in
her, because now she was living in a world made up of only her and
this guy. Once I found all this out, I wrote down the man's name
and cell phone number and phoned him.

"I'm Mrs. Terauchi's daughter," I told him straight out. "What
sort of relationship do you have with my mother?"

The guy didn't know what to say.

"I work under Mrs. Terauchi," he finally replied. "I'm happy to
be able to work with her, and respect her very much. That's the
only relationship we have."

So the man was a younger guy who worked at her office. I
remember Mom saying he was a nice guy, who had a daughter
Yukinari's age. I suddenly felt empty.

"I understand," I said. "That's fine."

I didn't ask my mom anything, so the man must have gotten in
touch with her about it, because she came to my room soon afterward and said, "It's not what you think. Don't worry, there's nothing between us."

Her eyes betrayed her, but I went ahead and nodded. I had all
the proof I needed. The e-mails. The fact that she didn't come
home. That sort of drunk look in her eyes. Those secretive conver-

sations on her cell phone. The curt, abrupt way she and Dad talked to each other.

But it never came to anything. I didn't want to lose my mother, so no matter how much pain and humiliation it involved, all I could do was give in. So I chose humiliation.

"It's okay. I get it," I said.

"Well, that's good to hear." She looked uneasy, but once she realized there wasn't anything left to talk about, she left my room.

Now, a year later, Mom's still coming home really late. Mom with her lies, me pretending not to notice. Maybe I'm being childish. No, that's not it. The last thing I want to hear is the sound of our relationship—Mom's and mine—cracking in two. I can't trust her, but I *have* to trust her to keep on going. Maybe I'll have to rework this whole trust thing.

I started to avoid Dad. The hatred I had for Mom spilled over to him. I couldn't express the hatred I felt for her directly, since I didn't want to lose her. Dad being Dad, he probably directed his own hatred for her toward me and my brother for the same reason. Back and forth with this twisted, misdirected hate, and it's choking me.

I've hidden my distrust of my mother and am doing my best to trust her and love her. But it might not work out. Because I love somebody I don't trust anymore, I've lost all faith in myself. I bet it's like this when parents abuse their children. Kids lose their trust in the parents they love, but still accept them, so they end up not trusting themselves anymore. Check it out, Worm. This is what I mean by something *irreparable*. Not murdering your mother.

. . .

I checked my watch. Eleven p.m. The air was smoggy, the sky around the sliver of moon all distorted. Mom still hadn't come back. I took a telephone card out of the desk drawer. Ever since I got a cell I haven't used telephone cards much and this one was unused, with a hundred units on it. I stuffed the house key, cell phone, and telephone card in my pocket, went out into the hallway, and listened to what was going on in the rest of the house. My kid brother was in his room, surfing the Web as usual, while Dad was snoring away in the living room, a lonely sort of sound.

Dressed in a T-shirt and shorts, I opened the door to our apartment. The night was muggy, without a breath of wind. Everybody must have been in bed in the neighborhood, because there was no one else out. But over in Karuizawa, Worm and Kirarin were still awake, planning how they were going to murder his father. In my heart, I'd murdered my own mother long ago, over and over.

I walked down the road, looking for a pay phone, my sandals slapping as they stuck to the hot asphalt. The road still hadn't cooled down. There were two pay phones, one next to the other, in front of the station. They were lit by a faint bank of fluorescent lights, and three taxis were lined up beside them, waiting for fares. Would they be able to trace the call? I turned around and looked for a pay phone in some darker corner of the neighborhood and spotted one next to a convenience store. Through the plate-glass front of the store, I could see several customers milling around among the rows of goods. I took a deep breath and pulled out the phone card.

"This is nine-one-one. What's your emergency?"

A middle-aged guy's nasal voice, full of suspicion. I took the plunge and spoke.

"I have something I want to tell you about the boy who killed his mother with a bat."

"What is it you want to report?"

I noticed, with a bit of happiness, how his tone of voice turned serious.

"I know where the boy is right now. I heard that he's hiding out in a vacant cottage in Karuizawa."

"And what is your name?"

"I can't tell you."

I hurriedly hung up. I had to get out of there or else they'd trace the call. I was concerned about leaving fingerprints on the receiver, but figured what'd it matter—when Worm and Kirarin got taken into custody, they'd check their call list and find my name on it, anyway. I hadn't given the police Kirarin's name, though, hoping that somehow she'd escape before Worm got caught.

When I got back to our apartment building, there was somebody standing in front of the elevator. My mom. She had on a black sleeveless sweater and white slacks. When I got near her I noticed a soapy fragrance that wasn't the smell of the soap we use at home. I averted my face.

"What are you doing out this late?" she asked.

"I made a call and ratted out somebody."

My mom turned pale when she heard this.

"Who did you call?"

"Does it matter?"

I slipped my arm inside my mom's stiffened arm. I really shouldn't hurt her, I thought.

Around nine p.m. we went into a small ramen shop along Highway 18. I wanted to go into a regular family-style restaurant, but brightly lit places like that would only show how shabby Worm looked and I didn't feel like going there with him. I guess I *was* starting to act pretty cruel to him. To me, Worm was a fallen idol.

The AC in the ramen place was going full blast and was so cold I got goose bumps. My bare arms were freezing. But the cold didn't bother me as much as my hunger, which tortured me and had me gulping back my saliva. Worm was just sitting there drinking a glass of water, but I was starving and ordered two bowls of pork ramen.

Since last night, Worm's been moping around, but I've been feeling great.

They passed the bowls of ramen to us across the counter. I did like guys do and sprinkled in a lot of garlic flakes and red pepper, pulled over the bowl of minced scallions and red pickled ginger and dumped in some of those as well. Mixed in everything in sight that was edible and then stirred it all together with my chopsticks. From the light pink soup I untangled some of the noodles. Even before I could stuff some in, my mouth was watering so badly that drops of saliva plopped down into the bowl. I've never been so starved in my life. I was impatient to gulp it all down but controlled myself and sipped some of the soup. I started to sweat and wiped this away with my hand, downing the noodles without chewing them. I was so desperately hungry it was a while before I even began to taste how good the ramen was.

I left home yesterday in the early afternoon, so this was the first food I'd had in over thirty hours. No wonder it tasted so good. Normally I never touch the fat on the pork slices, but now I gobbled it all down. I ate it all—the pickled ginger with its unnatural red color and all the additive-laden soup as well, glistening with fat under the fluorescent lights. But Worm, seated next to me, just sat there, staring at his bowl, disposable chopsticks still stuck together.

"What's the matter?"

I didn't ask this out of kindness but because I figured if he didn't have an appetite I could help myself to his ramen. He didn't reply.

"If you're not going to eat that, let me have it."

Worm had been spacing out but now he stared at me. He looked at me like, "Are you still here?" Of course I am, I thought. *You're* the one who kidnapped me, remember? You're the one who assaulted me back at the love hotel, so what the hell are you *talking* about? But Worm had no confidence—he was clumsy, slow on the uptake, didn't have enough guts to seduce me, a lousy kisser, plus he couldn't even get me naked. A total loser. An absolute clumsy oaf. Damn. Why was I wasting my time with a guy like this, anyway? I despised him and had already lost all interest. The cool-looking Worm pedaling away under the blazing sun had long since disappeared.

Last night, all that threatening me and making fun of me made him a little nuts. He was able to get on top of me, but once I stiffened up and he realized he wasn't going to get anywhere, he suddenly yelled out:

"Why can't things ever go my way?!"

"Of course they're not going to," I said. "What do you expect?"

I was pissed. I mean, come *on*. When had things ever gone the way I wanted them to in *my* life? The guys who try to pick me up are all jerks, and the guys I do like won't give me the time of day. That's the way it is for everybody—running back and forth between desire and reality, tossed about by life. All of a sudden it made me really angry to have someone like Worm make fun of me, to have a lowlife like him put me down.

"I wouldn't sleep with you even if you threaten me with your butcher knife," I said. "I'd rather die first. You're the biggest loser I've ever met. Hurry up and kill me already."

I was sure I was about to get stabbed, but instead I just heard this pitiful voice.

"How come?"

In an instant the tables had turned. I sat up and sent him flying. Worm fell headfirst onto the grubby stained carpet. I sneered at how stupid he looked. I felt full of courage and power and yelled some more.

"What the hell do you think you're doing, you virgin! I only sleep with cool guys. You're stupid and gross. If you wanna kill me like you did your mom, then be my guest. If that's what you have to do, go for it. It's easy. Blood will spurt out, I'll suffer, and die, that's it. I'll die hating you. So go ahead—I couldn't care less. I decided to come see a jerk like you, so I'm responsible. Which makes me different from Terauchi."

Worm was silent, crouched down in the dark. Soon I heard sobbing. What a wimp, I thought. Blubber away. I pulled out the flat box from his backpack that had the butcher knife. The source of his pointless confidence. The guiding principle behind his stupid hopes and dreams. I let the box, knife still inside, slip down in the space between the bed and the wall. No way I was going to let him straddle this bed again. Or get hold of the knife.

"You're such a loser," I went on. "You killed your mother, won me over, acted all cute with Terauchi, and said you're going to go murder your father. You think girls are all pretty dumb, don't you, and you're so much brighter. The whole world revolves around you. What a total jerk."

"Don't—don't be stupid." Worm moaned listlessly. He raised his pointy chin at me. "So what do you want me to do?"

"I'm going to phone my old boyfriend and I want you to threaten him. If you do a good job, I'll give your butcher knife back. And I'll pay for the hotel."

"But what should I say?"

Worm had turned into a good-for-nothing robot. I was ecstatic that I was the one pulling the strings now. It feels good when some guy with an inflated ego gets cut down to size. I felt I could do anything now—no matter how dumb, low, or evil. I picked up the old-fashioned phone from beside the bed. It was this awful pearl pink. I pushed the number for an outside line and punched in the phone number, which I still had memorized. Wataru's cell phone.

"When this guy named Wataru comes on," I explained, "tell him this. Say: 'You jerk. If you don't watch out, I'm gonna kill you. Better go see if your older sister's back home safe and sound. And your girlfriend—her, we're gonna gang-rape. So you better watch your step!'"

I didn't have time to check whether Worm had gotten all that, 'cause I was dying to hear Wataru's voice. The voice I still loved.

"Hello. Who is it? Hello? What number is this?"

I suppressed the desire to hear more of his voice and shoved the phone toward Worm. He hesitated at first but after I urged him on, he spewed out all this in a low voice:

"Is this Wataru? Me? I'm a murderer. No kidding. I offed my old lady. It's true. Smacked her with a bat. Crushed her skull good.

You can't say you haven't heard about it. It's in the papers—check it out. What about you? Ever killed somebody? I doubt it. Me, I'm screwing your old girlfriend right now. You don't know who I'm with? She hates your guts. She wants to kill you. You and your whole family—your old man, old lady, your sister, and your precious girl and all your buddies—she says she wants to annihilate the lot of them. Since you betrayed her, she says she wants you to vanish from the face of the earth. That's her one desire in life. And she wants me to do it for her. You listening, Wataru? Yep, damn right, I'm serious. Bet you didn't know someone wanted you dead this much. You thought you were just like any other guy, huh? Don't make me laugh. After I heard what you did, I'm definitely gonna kill the lot of you. So you better prepare yourself, ya jerk."

At first I thought, Serves him right, as I listened to this, but Worm went on and on and it started to creep me out. Signaling him we should hang up, I grabbed away the phone and found Wataru had hung up a long time ago. What an ass.

"He hung up. Redial it."

I punched in the number. At this point I didn't care whether they traced the call or he reported us to the police or whatever. No matter how much I let it ring, though, Wataru didn't pick up. Damn—I started to feel really upset and took it out on Worm.

"It's all your fault," I said. "You got me involved and it's made me twisted. You're the root of all evil, you know that? You're the cause of all this trouble. I've had it. I'm going home. Back to the ordinary world you'll never be able to return to."

"The world I can't return to?" he said. "You mean I've been kicked out?"

Worm raised his head and gave me a hard look. In the dark, his eyes glittered.

"But you're the one who decided to leave that world," I said.

Worm sighed. "I'm—frightened," he said. "Please—I need you to stay with me."

This was the second time Worm had surrendered. What a wimp. How could I not feel superior? Worm was weak, and I was strong—it was as simple as that. This night had been a turning point that had really changed me. I felt victorious, like I'd defeated an enemy. But still I was kind of uneasy. Maybe I'd entered Worm's world after all. Maybe that's why I'd made that threatening call to Wataru. But—was this really me? Was I really such an awful person?

I was just about finished eating, but Worm was still slumped over his bowl of ramen.

"I just realized I don't have an appetite."

" 'Cause you're thinking about your mother, I bet," I said sarcastically, in a low voice. "You regret what you did and it scares you."

Worm was facing me, but his eyes were elsewhere.

"I wonder. I—don't know."

"I don't really care one way or the other," I said, "but what happened to all the military talk?"

"Too much trouble."

Adrenaline surged through me. "I'll take that," I said, and switched my empty ramen bowl with his full one. This was the first time in my life I'd grabbed someone else's food. My parents always led a pretty well-off life, so good table manners were a kind of duty I'd been brought up with. *Eat all your meat, don't leave any carrots.* You know the drill. Mom always trimmed all the fat from our beef and pork and removed the skin from chicken. Snacks were homemade cookies or pudding, and she always made a homemade lunch for me to take to school. I didn't like egg yolks, so Mom always made me special fried eggs using just the whites. But right now, I was a total brat. I held on to the bowl of ramen Worm hadn't touched and thought, Yes! A strange idea came to me: Is this the kind of girl I really am? Meaning what happened last night, too.

With nothing else to occupy him, Worm sat there, engrossed in the TV. A program was on featuring NaiNai. A commercial for Geos came on next, with Okamura speaking English, but Worm still stared at the screen, like he was fascinated by it. I could understand what he was feeling. Like he was watching a world that he had no connection with anymore. The greasy TV set itself sat on top of this tacky colored box, the kind you could pick up in a supermarket. The cabinet was stuffed with dog-eared manga magazines that the other customers—young guys, truck drivers by the look of them, and the older guy, an outdoorsy type who looked like he ran the local motel—picked up and took back to their seats.

"Something's wrong with you, you know that?" I said.

"What do you mean?"

"It's like you've totally lost your confidence."

"No way."

Worm acted all tough, but when it came to breaking into a cottage he made a mess of it. He's the one who suggested that we sneak into a vacant cottage and stay there for a while, but I was the one who actually picked it out. I picked a pretty one with a nice red roof. But just when we broke the window of the bathroom with a rock, this earsplitting siren went off and a caretaker showed up in a four-wheel-drive car. How was I to know that cottages in the mountains had security systems?

We raced back down the mountain road in the dark. We finally came out on the highway but had nowhere to go to. We only had about ten thousand yen left and didn't want to spend it on a love hotel again, and using a vacant cottage hadn't worked out. That's when Worm started acting like all his batteries had given out. He stopped that stupid pretending-to-be-a-soldier routine, and his eyes got all vacant. You've got to eat something, I told him, and tried to comfort him by offering to pay for dinner. No matter what spin I might put on it, the reason I didn't take off for home right then and there was 'cause I found it interesting to watch Worm's steady decline. Or maybe I should say I enjoyed twisting Worm around my little finger. I never realized I had this streak of cruelty in me. Maybe what I really regretted about my relationship with Wataru was that I wouldn't have *him* under my thumb. So there was this side of me I never knew about before. And I was start-ing to think that maybe I liked it. A Kirarin who's stronger than anybody else. Stronger than Toshi, than Yuzan, than Terauchi. A woman who was *bad*. Maybe I'd finally discovered my real identity.

"As soon as you're done, let's get out of here." Worm poked me in the side with his elbow. His elbow grazed my breast, and I frowned.

"Knock it off, you pervert. I don't want anything to do with you."

"Sorry," he apologized meekly.

"Where're we going when we leave?" I asked.

"To a convenience store. I like them."

Worm looked uncomfortably around the interior of the ramen shop. We paid for the food, and when we went outside the sky was full of stars. We hadn't noticed before, maybe because it was still a little light out. I gazed up at the night sky, a mountain in my peripheral vision. It was Mount Asama. I couldn't see the whole mountain—it was like some huge monster crouching there, melting into the dark. A mountain like that at night is awful. It reminded me of Worm last night, crouched by the bed, his eyes glittering in the darkness. The guy is definitely weird, I thought, and shuddered. Deep down, I wanted to get away from him.

"Do you think I should kill my dad?" Worm asked me as we trudged along the highway, heading toward a convenience store we could see lit up in the distance.

"If you wanna kill him, then why not? It's got nothing to do with me. You have to do it, otherwise you won't feel like you got back at him, right?"

"Yeah, I suppose. Yeah, I guess you're right. But I don't understand why I have to murder to settle a score. Why do you think that is?"

Worm had become totally introspective and moody. And I'd turned arrogant. Go figure.

"Don't ask me. It's something you have to settle yourself. So why did you kill your mother? She's the one who gave birth to you. So you didn't want to be anybody's child anymore?"

Worm came to a halt and let out a deep breath. His loneliness came to me like a vibration in the air, but I turned away from him to show him I wasn't buying it. Worm, in his own world. Everybody else is still in *my* world. Everybody except Wataru, that is. Last night I was sure I was in Worm's world, but I was wrong. I hadn't killed anybody. I felt kind of relieved. In the dark I could hear Worm muttering.

"You're exactly right, Kirarin. Maybe what I want is to cut all ties with everybody. The thread or something that keeps me connected to the world, the worthless proof that I exist."

The instant I heard him say my name I had a weird feeling. An uneasy sense. *This side—the other side.* Which one was I on? As I walked along in the darkness of this plateau, hemmed in by mountains, I wasn't sure.

All of a sudden my cell rang. The orange display lit up the

sender's name: *Wataru*. Maybe he realized it was me calling last night. Worm, up ahead, turned around and shot me a suspicious look. Trying to keep my heart from racing, I answered the phone.

"It's me. Wataru. You okay?" I missed him so much I was about to tear up.

"Yeah, I'm fine," I said. "It's been a long time. Maybe a year and a half?"

My voice naturally got higher. Worm was standing a little ways off, looking in my direction.

"Yeah, I think that's about right. You have college entrance exams coming up next year, right?"

Wataru was in college already, in the law department at Waseda. Which is why I was originally thinking of trying for Waseda myself, but now I'd given that up and decided to settle for some junior college. My guilty conscience was making it hard for me to get the words out.

"That's right," I said.

"You preparing for it?"

"I guess . . ."

"Well, good luck with it. You know something? Last night I got this weird phone call. I thought maybe it had something to do with you, so I started to get worried about you."

"What kind of call?" I asked.

"Never mind. I don't want to talk about it. It was just a prank call, but I got concerned, hoping nothing terrible had happened to you."

"You were worried about me? That makes me happy."

My eyes started to well up. I still like you, Wataru. I *love* you. I felt so sad and lonely it hurt. I felt guilty, too, for the ugly thing I'd done out of jealousy. The thing I'd done that had soiled this shining person, Wataru.

"But why are you worried?" I asked. "Nothing's happened to me."

"The guy who called mentioned the girl I used to go out with, and you're the only one. He said it quite clearly—*your old girl-friend*. So I thought he had to have something to do with you. I thought maybe you'd gotten mixed up with some weird guy. But if you're okay, that's great."

At this moment it hit me: I'd lost Wataru forever. He's the one who told me he loved me the best of all, so why didn't I trust him anymore? I wanted to talk with him some more and was searching for the right words when he said, "Well, see you," and hung up. Devastated, I stared at the screen. The whole call had lasted only three minutes and twenty seconds.

"Who was it?" Worm asked.

"None of your business."

He was annoyed, and out of spite he called Terauchi. It's okay, I thought. I get it. We're not going out or anything, so when it's just the two of us it's like I can't breathe. I need air. I knew it was stupid, but I couldn't shake this sadness and I got more and more depressed. Here I was, walking in the dark, in this place I've never been, with a guy I just met. What's the matter with me, anyway?

Worm made a show of being all cheerful as he talked with Ter-auchi. The idiot. "I want it to be really original," he was telling her. He was discouraged but tried to put on a brave front. While he was talking I got on with Terauchi. She told me she'd seen Worm's photo on the Internet. In the *other* world. The world where Wataru was, and Terauchi, and Toshi. The world of exams, hook-ing up with guys, Shibuya, friends. I can't go back anymore, Ter-auchi. That's what I felt, but I forced myself to sound all bouncy and cheerful as I talked with her, trying to stand the pain of losing Wataru, of being banished from their bright world forever.

Next we stopped by a convenience store, bought some boxed lunches and drinks, and stood for a while leafing through magazines. Worm took a bath last night at the love hotel, but he was smelly already. I was worried I was starting to smell, too. I might not share in his guilt but was starting to think there were some things the two of us shared. As we left the store, I grabbed a can of deodorant and spritzed my underarms when no one was looking. Just then I got a text message from Teru.

Kirarin, what's going on? You've got me worried. Give me a call.

Too much trouble to tell the truth, so I lied: *I'm back home now. I'll tell you all about it later. Don't forget the concert next week. Not to worry—I'm fine.*

Why was I starting to find Teru a nuisance? I'd always been proud of having this nice gay friend whom I could tell anything to. But I'd only been using his friendship for my own purposes. When I was with him it looked like I was with a guy, but it was totally safe and fun. Who knows—maybe having a high school girl as a friend was something he was proud of, too. A typical party girl like me. It had always been a light kind of relationship, where you didn't share any of your pain or sadness. If Teru had really been a friend, I might have answered him like this: "Being with Worm I don't know up from down anymore. I always thought I was a good person, but maybe I'm really bad. Maybe even a worse person than Worm. Hey, can you lend me some money?"

"I want you to go home."

I was staring at the cell phone when Worm, standing behind me, muttered this. I turned around.

"How come?"

"It's pointless for you to be with me. Besides, I'm a criminal."

The whites of his slanty eyes stood out as he stared at me. And all of a sudden, out of nowhere, I realized that the last thing I wanted to do was go home. A weird feeling—like on the one hand I wanted to go back to that *other* world, but at the same time didn't care if my connections to it were cut forever. It wasn't a feeling of being free or anything. I just didn't want to go back. I wanted to float somewhere in between.

"But last night you said you wanted me to stay with you," I said.

"So you want to be with me?"

"Not particularly."

Worm walked on, the plastic bag from the convenience store swishing with each step. And I followed behind him.

I started to notice that there were a lot of cops around as we were walking along a mountain road toward more cottages thinking we'd try to break into another one. Two patrol cars, one after the other, drove up the road from the foothills. The second one stopped in front of the nearest cottage, and a policeman got out and buzzed the intercom. Worm and I were hiding in a thicket of bamboo grass and he nudged me.

"This is bad. Doesn't look like they're just after some sneak thief. Somebody must have ratted us out."

"But who'd do that?" I asked.

"Your friends. They all know about me. Maybe Yuzan. I don't like her much and I acted kind of cold to her."

All of a sudden, Terauchi's laid-back voice came to me. Whenever she talks that calmly it means she's up to something. Only when she's trying to hide her real intentions does she tell all those stale jokes and act dumb.

Dude. Sounds like you and the murderer are getting along just fine.

I hear you're in Karuizawa?

"It's got be Terauchi!" I yelled. "I'm sure of it. Toshi and Yuzan both helped you escape. They wouldn't turn you in. Terauchi's the only one who didn't help out."

"So that's the kind of person she is?"

Worm looked despondent. Maybe he was regretting giving her that childish order to write his criminal manifesto.

"I don't know," I said. "The others I can read, but not her. She's the only one who's unpredictable."

Which means I don't trust her, I guess. For the first time in my life, I felt like I understood the relationship between Terauchi and me.

"Damn," I said. "We're in for it now."

I tried calling Terauchi but her phone was turned off. That settled it. I had to get out of there. I panicked. I had to escape, no matter what. I mean, if they arrested me now I'd be stuck in *this world* forever. Floating is fine, but getting stuck isn't. Before anyone even realized it, I wouldn't be able to go back to the other world—the one Wataru lived in. The world where the sun shines. But why was Terauchi trying to get me shut away like this? There's a moment with her when a kind of severe look crosses her nice features, the kind of look that keeps everybody out. No way, Terauchi! I won't forget what you've done! I was burning with hatred.

"What should we do?" Worm said.

I looked at him. He laid his backpack down in the bushes, tilted his long neck to one side, lost in thought. We don't have time for that, I thought, and grabbed his arm.

"We've got to decide right now," I said. "If we don't do something we're going to get caught."

"I know, I know. But I just can't think of anything."

"Let's stay over at a cheap love hotel and take a train back to

Tokyo tomorrow morning. If it's a local train we should be able to afford it."

"But where're we going to go when we get back?" Worm tossed his boxed lunch on the ground. "I killed my old lady, remember? I don't have anyplace to go."

"Then let's go kill your dad, too."

I clung to Worm's ridiculous plan. Instead of debating what was right and wrong, I wanted to get moving and *do* something. That's all it was.

"You'd kill my dad with me?"

I shook my head.

"No. 'Cause I don't hate him."

My mind wasn't working anymore. I stood there, feeling like I'd lost everything. A mosquito landed on my bare leg, but it was too much trouble to brush it away. As I sat there vacantly, Worm suddenly hugged me to him. "You stink, you idiot," I told him. I tried to push him away, but he held me tight and wouldn't let me go. We plopped down into the bushes. The stems of the bamboo grass poked me. It hurts, I was about to say, but before I could, Worm had mashed his lips against mine, rough and strong. I was faceup and he made a grab for my breasts. The moment I decided he could do whatever he wanted with me, the pain turned to pleasure. I pulled up my T-shirt and took off my own clothes. I was on fire, the first time I'd ever felt that way. How could we be doing something like this, I thought, when we'd been driven into a corner? We laid our clothes down on the ground to lie on, then had wild, frantic sex.

"I'm hungry."

Worm, naked, was looking around to locate the box lunch he'd thrown away earlier. He finally found it and came back to where I was. He'd suddenly gotten all kind and gentle, and it made me happy. Naked, we ate the lunch together, taking turns swigging sips from the water bottle. After that we did it again, this time standing up with me leaning back against the trunk of a tree. I felt like I was doing it with him forever.

Suddenly a flashlight shone above us and we heard men's voices. Maybe the police had heard us talking and had tracked us down. Were they combing the hills for us? We flattened ourselves against the ground, avoiding the light. What would we do if they found us? I was scared out of my mind. Not of being chased by adults, but of being discovered like this in the hills, naked, having sex, being scolded and accused. It was a feeling close to original sin. Like Adam and Eve.

"Let's get out of here," Worm whispered.

I threw my clothes on; then Worm grabbed my hand and we raced down the mountain path. Every time a car or patrol car passed we hid beside the road in the bushes. When we finally reached Highway 18, there was a patrol car outside the convenience store we'd stopped at.

Just then an empty cab drove up. If I let that cab get away, I thought, I'll never escape this world.

"Let's take that cab back to Tokyo," I said.

"We don't have enough money."

I looked Worm in the face.

"Didn't you tell me you were going to rob a cab?"

I ran out onto the highway and flagged down the cab. The cab slowed to a stop, and I could see a surprised look on the driver's face as Worm pushed me from behind.

"Let's do it."

We climbed in the back of the cab. It was full of cigarette smoke and chilled by the AC. The driver, with his typical white cloth-covered cap, was obviously local, and he turned around slowly. An old guy in his late forties. A plastic bottle of tea lay on the seat beside him.

"When I just saw the girl I figured it was a ghost. So you're dating, huh?"

"That term's too old. We're not dating, we're a *couple*." My voice shook as I spoke, and I laughed to try to cover it up. "Excuse me, but we'd like to go to Tokyo. We have to get back to Tokyo right away."

"To Tokyo at this time of night?"

"There aren't any more trains, and someone is very sick, so we've got to get back. Please let us out in Chōfu, at the Chōfu exit."

The driver checked out Worm in the rearview mirror and looked startled for a second. Did he know who we were? Worried, I looked over at Worm, who was staring down, his face pale. You jerk. Get it together. I kicked him on the foot.

"It's his father," I explained. "He's on his deathbed. So, please, take us there."

"I see," the driver said, his expression kinder. But his next question was anything but friendly. "I'm sorry to ask at a time like this, but do you have enough money? Night rates apply now and it should easily be fifty thousand yen to Tokyo."

"Don't worry. We have enough cash."

Still looking doubtful, the driver slowly started to pull away.

"I'm glad to hear that. I was just a little concerned, you being so young and all."

"Please just take us there. Don't worry, you'll get paid."

The driver pulled the cab over to the side of the road.

"Sorry, but would you mind showing me the cash?"

The driver's stubbornness really pissed me off. I had only ten thousand yen, so how in the world was I going to pay? Worm suddenly yelled, "If we don't have enough, my parents will pay the rest! So please—my dad's dying here."

Worm's yelling clearly pissed off the driver. And he stared hard at me, checking out how I looked. My T-shirt was muddy and covered with leaves. I quickly brushed them off.

"Miss, please don't do that. The cab will get all dirty."

At a loss for what to do, I glanced over at Worm. With one hand he was rustling around in his backpack on the floor. He'd taken the butcher knife back. I held down his arm and said in an insistent voice, "I'll phone home."

I had no choice, so I dialed home. As I expected, my mom, sounding sleepy, answered, grumbling right off the bat. "Where in the world are you? You didn't call, so I was worried. What are you doing out this late?"

"I'm on my way home, but don't seem to have enough for the taxi fare. When I get there, can you pay it?"

She was launching into another complaint, so I hurriedly hung up.

"She said they'll pay."

The taxi driver must have overheard my mom, so he nodded reluctantly and started to drive. Good—at least we'd get back to Tokyo. I felt optimistic—as long as we got back there, something would work out. Then the *enka* song on the radio suddenly cut off and a voice came on, full of static.

"A customer has forgotten something in one of the cabs. Something very large. It's a young male customer. I repeat, a customer has forgotten something in one of the cabs. A young male customer. If anyone finds this large item, please get in touch right away."

The driver looked up into the rearview mirror. I felt uneasy.

"That was the police channel, wasn't it?" Worm asked.

"No, it's from our company."

The driver didn't look back anymore. He was driving at a leisurely pace. I drank the rest of the water from our plastic bottle. The bottom of the bottle was muddy, so I wiped it on the seat. Now *this* was an adventure! My confusion I felt before about having sex with Worm in the woods had vanished, and I was happy with how bold we'd been. As I stared at the taillights of the car in front of us, I got sleepy, and finally started to doze off.

"What the hell do you think you're doing?"

At Worm's voice, I jolted awake. The butcher knife was right in front of my eyes, its point aimed at the driver's neck.

"What happened?" I asked.

"This jerk was going to pull into a police station."

Flustered, I looked outside and saw a police station pass by on the left side. The driver, looking upset, was facing straight ahead. "You guys better knock it off," he muttered. "Robbing a cab is a felony. You've got to think of your future."

Worm just sneered at him. "I don't have a future, buddy. I murdered my old lady."

The driver gulped. The butcher knife glittered as the lights from passing cars shone in on us. We were nearing the highway intersection. Several cars were lined up, including a patrol car near the entrance. "They've set up a checkpoint!" I yelled to Worm.

"Take the frontage road," he commanded the driver.

Reluctantly, the driver turned off onto the side road, a country road lined with drive-ins. "You won't be able to escape forever," the driver said in a pitiful voice. "I'm not trying to trick you or anything, but I think you should stop it. I'll give you my money, but just get out of here, okay? You're still young."

"Shut up and drive," Worm replied.

"Where to?"

"I told you a million times, you idiot—to Tokyo!"

The driver clammed up and the taxi continued down the narrow road. The driver's cell phone suddenly rang, and I was surprised by the melody, the fanfare signaling the start of a horse race. "Don't answer it," Worm ordered, and the driver nodded in resignation. The phone rang one more time, but he ignored it. After about fifteen minutes, Worm said to me, "Hold the knife for a while. I'm getting tired."

He handed me the butcher knife and sank back, exhausted, onto the seat. With a trembling hand I took the handle. Worm must have been pretty tense, because the grip was slippery with sweat. The driver glanced at the knife and then looked straight at me. Miss, stop what you're doing, his eyes pleaded with me. I held on to the knife tightly with both hands and pointed it at the driver's throat. An old guy's dirty throat with veins sticking out. I remembered, when I was a freshman in high school, how middle-aged guys in Shibuya used to call out to me, trying to pick me up.

Hey, how 'bout a cup of tea?

They were such grungy old guys that it made me wonder how they could possibly pick up young girls. Cigarette breath, shabby suits, at most ten thousand or twenty thousand yen on them. They could try to pick us up, girls the same age as their own daughters, because they thought we were fools. Their daughters were in this nice world, they thought, but girls like me were in a fallen world. They made a clear distinction between the two. All of a sudden, I got good and steamed and pressed the knifepoint, which hadn't been touching the driver, right up against his wrinkled throat.

"Miss, that's a little too close. You're scaring me," the driver begged.

"No way. Don't screw with me."

"I'm not. I'm asking because it makes it hard to drive. If we got into an accident here you'd be the ones who'd regret it. I don't know what you guys did, but you're going to get in a lot of trouble."

I was enraged. He didn't seem afraid, even with the knife to his throat. He really wasn't scared. Beside me, Worm sat up.

"I was just about to call it a night," the driver said, "so when you said drive you all the way to Tokyo I wasn't too happy about it. But at the same time, I thought if you really were in a bind, I'd help you out. Taxi drivers are generally pretty good people, you know. But it really pisses them off to get threatened by punks like you. Me, too. I was thinking of doing this, and I don't care if I get hurt."

Suddenly he started zigzagging the car back and forth. I fell over on Worm's lap and the knife dropped onto the floor. The driver kept on weaving back and forth. Worm and I were tossed left and right, our bodies smashing into each other. A truck coming in the other direction blasted his horn and barely managed to slip by.

"What the hell do you think you're doing?!"

Worm picked up the butcher knife and sliced it across the driver's throat. Blood spurted out, and I couldn't stop scream-ing, "Stop it! Stop it!" But I had no idea what it was I wanted to stop. Probably not Worm cutting the driver's throat—instead, I was furious that the driver was swerving all over the place. You idiot! Stop making fun of me! You dirty old men. And Terauchi. And Wataru.

"I'm not going to stop. I told you I don't care if I get hurt."

The driver unsnapped his seat belt. The taxi continued to race down the road, veering over into the opposite lane. We passed a motorcycle and zoomed up a road into the hills.

"I told you to knock it off!" Worm screamed. I grabbed the driver's hair from behind to get him to stop, but the plastic screen got in the way. His white cloth-covered cap flew off. At the same time a stream of red blood sprayed against the windshield. I was covered in hot blood—the hideous, filthy blood of an old man. I screamed. And then we crashed hard into something and I felt myself flying off somewhere. Flying through the sky. Such a wonderful, wonderful feeling.

D ear Ninna Hori,
        Or maybe I should say "Dear Miss Toshiko Yama-
        naka"? Or maybe "Dear Toshi-chan—I love you"?

I'm writing to you, Toshi, because you're the only one I can tell
this to. I know you might get mad and say, "What a thing to say!"
But I know you'll also sympathize with me and say that Terauchi
must be a pretty lonely person. And that's fine. Both are true, so
please listen to me.

By the time this letter gets to you tomorrow morning, I won't
be here in the world anymore. I know starting out the letter like
this makes it sound like some dark manga or dumb novel, and I
bet it'll disappoint you. But it's true. As soon as I mail the letter
I'm planning to die. I'm going to die right away because I think it
would be a lousy thing if you heard about my death before you got
this letter, and I want to avoid that at all costs. By the way, I actually did try writing a dumb novel like this with a similar opening
line, but the thing turned out to be the pits, so I crumpled it all
up, ripped it into a million pieces, and flushed it down the toilet
along with my pee.

This is the first and last serious letter I'll ever write to you,
Toshi, and I wish I could stop hiding, but it's like that's all I can do
anymore. Still, I feel sorry for myself and feel awful about vanish-
ing from this life, and I'm writing this as a kind of pep talk to tell
myself I've got to have the guts to do it, and I'm having this
dilemma about how I can possibly convey to you the struggle I'm
going through. Words are such a pain, so sluggish I feel like rip-
ping my tongue right out. But if you think about it, writing this
puts it into words, but since I'm not telling you directly, in person,

my struggle is not so much about words as it is about *me*. That's right—I'm still afraid of being totally honest. I'm more afraid of this than dying. So what am I doing getting all shy about something like writing, huh?

Okay, I've finally calmed down a bit. If you say I hide things because I'm shy, that can't be right. I've finally realized it's for a different reason—that I don't want to see the darkness that lies in my heart. And this agony I've been going through as I try to figure out what I want to tell you in this letter, Toshi—I finally understand the reason I'm writing. I'm really a dismal excuse for a person. But I'm so tense and nervous, hoping I can somehow communicate to you, Toshi, about the kind of person I am.

I know this is a roundabout way of talking, but that's the way my thoughts work, spiraling round and round. My mind works like that, too, but the conclusion is surprisingly simple. All I want is for someone to understand me before I die. With death staring me in the face, I finally understand the reason novelists write books: before they die they want somebody, somewhere, to understand them. In my case this isn't my mother, or father, or Yukinari, or Yuzan. It's just you, Toshi-chan.

I know you may find this a pain, but I want to wipe the slate clean before I die, so please read this. If you don't want to, could you just stop here? Even if you don't want to read it yourself, that's cool, but whatever you do, don't show it to my mother, okay? Just keep what you've read so far in your heart and throw it away.

I'm sorry if this is a burden for you. But I'm so happy I met you, Toshi. If I hadn't, I'd have died without revealing to anyone the darkness inside of me. This might sound all pure and righteous, but it isn't. The reason is that I need to die, but only after really taking a good hard look at myself and seeing what kind of person I am. Do you see what I mean? And to do that, you need somebody else's eyes to look at you. So please, Toshi, see through to the *real me,* be brave, and laugh. Say, "What a jerk she was, that Terauchi! A girl like her leaving the world? Well, I say good riddance!" Is that asking too much?

If our positions were reversed and you were in my shoes, I would definitely do that. I promise you I would. You might think that's kind of a sneaky thing to say, to talk about something impossible like making a promise to you even though I'm dying first. But there's nothing sneaky about it. Because I'm exposing things I've dragged out while you weren't aware of it. You've changed me, little by little, Toshi. So we're in the same boat. What I mean is, you have to deal with my death.

I don't think you understand at all why I'm going to die, so let me explain a little. That's only fair. There are a couple of reasons why I can't go on living anymore.

One is my difficult personality. I think you know about that. I'm this superphilosophical kind of person. Stuck in a prison of abstract ideas and overpowering emotions, I have this personality that makes it really hard to survive. Plus, I'm living in the middle of a familiar transformation, I guess you'd call it, something mankind's never experienced before, with the role of the family getting more messed up than anybody imagines, changing day by day, growing more and more complicated and individualistic, something nobody can really comprehend, and I have to pretend to fill all these roles every day. Otherwise I can't survive. That totally wears me out. In the reality of everyday occurrences I've had to submit to people in order not to lose them.

It's less the submission that bothers me, I guess, than how it makes my life miserable. And what happens if I can't forgive myself for making that choice? And what if, in order to keep on living, I have to continue to accept myself? What am I supposed to do? Conclusion: It'd be best if I'm destroyed. The best thing is for me to just vanish.

By the way, the person who's caused me so much grief is some-one you've met before, Toshi—my mother. A mother complex? Sorry, that's not it. I've already gone beyond that. Still, as a per-son, I like her. I don't want to make her suffer, yet I've turned into this old person who shouldn't outlive her.

There's one more major reason that I don't want to—can't—go on living. There's something I have to take responsibility for. Kirarin's accident. The accident in which Kirarin and that taxi driver from Nagano died, and in which Worm was critically injured. It's all my fault.

After I die, nobody will be able to discover the truth, so I want to set it down clearly here. The night Worm and Kirarin phoned me I told the police where they were. I made an anonymous call from a public phone at a convenience store in front of the station and told the police that they were in a vacant cottage in Karuizawa. That's why Worm and Kirarin tried to escape the police dragnet by robbing a taxi, which led to the accident. So something that never should have happened did, all because of my thoughts and actions. A clear-cut cause-and-effect relation-ship. I was the one who caused it, and I should probably get the death penalty. Or maybe what I should say is I'm the one who pronounced the death sentence on *myself*.

I can hear you saying, Toshi, that I shouldn't feel responsible. But, like some criminal who's convinced that what he's doing is right, I ran Kirarin and Worm into a corner and tried to punish them. That's a fact. I despised Worm because he ran away from something that *can't be undone* and chose the easy way out of something that *can* be. Which for him was killing his mother. He chose the easy path and then ran away, and I despised him for it.

I love my mother too much and so I forgave her, but I hated myself for forgiving her, and started to hate myself so much that I didn't want to be in this world anymore. At the same time I burned with hatred for Worm, for the hostility he had toward his mother. 'Cause what he did didn't involve my kind of roundabout thinking. It evaded thinking, actually. It was just too simple. I was angry because he boiled down his trouble into a very simplistic response. I think I started to apply this weird logic to Kirarin, too. Needless to say, I was also angry at you, Toshi, for hesitating to report Worm to the police, and at Yuzan for lending him her bike. Still I pretended as always to be casually helping out Worm and Kirarin. I wonder why. Maybe I'm evil, after all.

After I phoned the police I felt awful, like I had something bitter in my mouth that I couldn't get rid of, no matter how much I swallowed. Now I realize that taste came to me the instant I crossed the line. That night I tried to avoid the whole thing, got into bed, and forced myself to shut my eyes, but then had lots of weird dreams. In one dream, Kirarin was riding in the back of a truck, going off to be sold somewhere. In another one, I reported my mother to the police. Wonder what Freud would say about that?

Then early the next morning I got a phone call from you. As soon as I heard you scream through the cell phone that Kirarin had died, I knew it. That what I had done had brought on a tragedy that could never be undone. For me the idea of something that can't be undone seemed an internal emotion, etched in the hearts of the living. But when I realized I'd lost Kirarin, that this was something *real* that truly was irreparable, I got goose bumps all over. I was terrified. Terror is more dangerous than the prospect of self-exposure; I could see my whole philosophy of life falling apart. The world I'd thought was real collapsed, and out of it another reality appeared. A meta-reality. I'd been pondering for a long time who I was and had almost reached a conclusion, but now I had to start again from scratch. I wonder if I was wrong.

I was acting strangely, so my mom asked me what was wrong. "Kirarin died in Karuizawa," I told her, "in an accident." My mother was shocked and said, "How could that happen? Her poor mother." What do you think I said back to her then, Toshi? A line that even now makes me blush. Something so dumb that would make this hyperphilosophical girl a complete laughingstock. No matter that this letter is my suicide note, it's too embarrassing to write down what I said to my mom. Out of consideration for our friendship, I hope you'll forgive me.

Anyhow, I'm ashamed of myself. And very, very tired. It seems like I've reached the right moment to die. I feel sorry for my mother, but she has someone more important in her life than me, so I'm sure she'll survive. Sorry, but I'm not thinking about my father and brother, either. I'm sure that for you, Toshi, getting this letter knowing I've died will be really tough. But you're a good person, with a strong, honest soul, and I know you'll be okay. Not me, though—I'm done for. I want to say good-bye to everybody. Hmm—sounds like something from Dazai Osamu, doesn't it? How pointless was that, writing reports for school? Bye-bye. I'm off on a journey to the real world. 'Cause within this meta-reality what's *real* is this—my death. You hang in there, now, okay? Later, dude.

Kazuko Terauchi

No doubt about it, this was a suicide note. I'd never held a suicide note, or read one, in my life. When I thought that these were Terauchi's last words, somehow I couldn't fathom what they all meant.

She ended up not actually mailing the letter. It was sealed, with my name on it, on top of her desk. It didn't have a stamp on it, so she must not have wanted to take the trouble to buy one. Instead she jumped off the roof of a nearby apartment building. Even though she'd made such a big deal about how she wanted the letter to arrive before the news of her death. Such impatience. Just that fact alone revealed how confused Terauchi had been. It made me want to laugh, but instead my face was all scrunched up in pain. *Come on, you dummy!* I wanted to say. *Get it right!*

Worm's mother's death, Kirarin's death, the death of that taxi driver, Worm's injury, Terauchi's suicide. Too many shocking things had happened one after another, and tears wouldn't come. I couldn't think about it deeply. Like an empty shell, I opened up Terauchi's last letter and had to read it with Terauchi's parents and my mother looking over my shoulder.

"What did she say?"

Terauchi's mother asked this the second I finished reading. In just half a day her face had turned dry and listless, drained of life. She looked desperate to know the reason why her daughter killed herself. Only Terauchi's father was sobbing—her mother was toughing it out. Yukinari, her younger brother, had shut himself in his room and refused to come out.

My mother rested her hand on my shoulder as if to protect me, and it felt heavy. Terauchi's mother had phoned us, saying, "There's a letter left behind addressed to Toshiko, so I'd like you to come over and open it." As soon as we heard this, we dropped everything and raced over.

I'd never imagined that I'd be hearing about Terauchi's death, and it was all so sudden and crazy that it was almost funny. That's why I couldn't cry. My heart just felt empty. To begin with, early that morning we'd gotten the shocking news of Kirarin's death and that turned into a huge uproar, not just in my house or the neighborhood, but with calls coming from school, too.

The female detective who'd questioned me before was the one who told me the news about Kirarin's death in the accident. And then, half a day later, this phone call telling us Terauchi had killed herself. So as I started to read her letter, I had no clue at all what it was all about. I was totally confused and tried my best to be calm.

This is how it all took place:

Early on the morning of August tenth, our home phone rang. It had to be either a salesman or a relative. Other people would just call each of our cell phones, which made a phone call coming in the morning all the more ominous. Nobody else was up yet, and I counted the rings as the phone echoed in the quiet house—one . . . two . . . Six thirty by my clock. It's got to be bad news, I thought, and tugged my blanket up to my chest. At the fifth ring it sounded like Dad answered it downstairs. No way. No way! The extension in my room rang, and it was Dad's voice.

"It's from the police. They want to talk to you."

I was pretty depressed, figuring they'd finally caught Worm and had learned how we'd helped him get away. I guess *depressed* isn't the right word. It was more like *Darn it all!* Racing to think up some excuses, I reluctantly came on the phone.

"Good morning. My apologies for calling so early." It was the female detective from before, and she was so polite it made me even more confused for a second.

"Toshiko? I apologize if you were sleeping," the woman went

on. "But something terrible has happened and I thought I should let you know. It will shock you, but please try to remain calm. It's hard for me to make this call. The Nagano Prefectural Police contacted us and informed us that a high school student named Miss Kirari Higashiyama passed away a short time ago in a hospital in Karuizawa. She was with the boy who lives next door to you, and I was really surprised, wondering how this happened. She goes to the same high school as you, so is she a friend of yours? I wonder if she had been seeing the boy next door before this. I'd appreciate it if you'd tell me whatever you know."

Kirarin was dead. I was totally shocked, and was sure that Worm must have killed her.

"Was Kirarin murdered?"

"By Kirarin you mean Miss Higashiyama?" the female detective asked calmly. "I don't have all the details, but we do know that your neighbor robbed a taxi late last night. The taxi was weaving back and forth and crashed into an oncoming car and was destroyed. Miss Higashiyama went through the windshield and was thrown onto the road. They said she was unconscious. She suffered trauma to her entire body and passed away. It's unclear why she was with the young man, but eyewitnesses state they seemed to be close. Please tell me what was going on."

The detective, it surprised me, was close to tears. A random thought sprang into my mind—the image of the heavy brooch pinned to her blouse. The fact that Kirarin was dead just wouldn't sink in.

"I have no idea," I said.

Which was true, I didn't have a clue. I might have known that Kirarin was with Worm, but why did she have to die? It made no sense. It was like some totally astonishing thing had just fallen from the sky and my world was suddenly in chaos.

"Is that so? Well, I guess we can talk about it more some other time."

She sounded resigned.

"How do you know they attacked a taxi?" I asked.

"The driver was cut with a knife and died from loss of blood. His throat was apparently cut. They must have cut him from behind. Your neighbor testified to this as well at the hospital."

Damn. This was awful. How could Worm take Kirarin with him and do something like that? I couldn't believe it. My knees started to shake and I couldn't stand. I collapsed onto the bed. Somebody tapped me on the shoulder. I looked up and Dad was there, holding out an opened newspaper to me. The headline read, "Runaway Assaults Taxi and Causes Accident." The news managed to make it into the morning paper. Neither Worm's nor Kirarin's name was given, but she was described as "the high school girl accompanying him," hinting at her being an accomplice.

"What happened to Worm—I mean the boy next door?" I asked the detective.

"He's got injuries on his right arm and head and broke some ribs, and was taken to the hospital." Maybe I was just imagining it, but her voice sounded cold. "They suspected some internal damage, as well, but I haven't heard anything after that. We're going there now to check on the situation."

As soon as she hung up, I dialed Kirarin's cell phone but only got her voice mail. What happened to her phone? When I pictured her little pink cell phone lying along the side of some road, it hurt. I dialed her home next, but it was the same thing—voice mail.

I looked at the curtain. I could sense, outside, the blue sky of morning. It looked like another hot summer day. Was this really happening? I couldn't believe it, and my mind was total confusion.

My father seemed to be saying something but I couldn't absorb it. Suddenly I realized I had to phone Terauchi. I jumped up to get my cell again, and when he saw this, Dad left my room.

If I hadn't phoned her, Terauchi might not have died that day.

"Terauchi, Kirarin's dead."

She didn't say anything.

"Did you hear me? Kirarin's dead."

"I heard you."

Her voice was so small and low it sounded like it was filtering up through the earth's core. How can she possibly be so calm? I wondered.

"I'm not kidding. The police just phoned me. Worm attacked a taxi driver and there was an accident. Kirarin was unconscious and died. Worm just broke some bones and survived. The driver died, too. They said his throat was cut. The two of them attacked the driver. What happened, do you think? Maybe they were trying to rob him? What should I do? What are you supposed to do in a situation like this?"

I got all this out in a rush of words and finally noticed Terauchi's silence.

"What's the matter, Terauchi? Did you hear what I said?"

She answered in this slow, casual way, "That's awful. That things ended up like that."

"Of course it's awful," I said. "But they're dead, and there's nothing we can do about that. I was so shocked when I heard. It's all my fault. What do you think?"

I was shaken, convinced I was to blame for the whole thing. I never told the police about my bike and cell phone being stolen. I'd gotten in touch with Worm a number of times after that, and even rooted for him to escape. All of us had been idiots. Criminals, even. Terauchi tried to cheer me up.

"There's no need for you to get all upset, Toshi. You didn't do anything so bad. I'm the one who did something bad."

"What do you mean?"

"I'm the one who changed fate, I guess."

Terauchi mumbled this puzzling thing. Then I heard this popping noise, like she was getting the kinks out of her neck.

"What's that sound?"

"I'm setting my alarm clock."

"You're going back to sleep?"

I couldn't believe how nervy she was. What she thought of all this, what she was thinking about, I didn't even try to imagine. Or even give it a thought. All I could think about was myself. About me and how the adults were going to blame me. Looking back on it now, I can see that when she set her clock she was setting a time limit for herself, for how much longer she had to live.

"That's right. I'm going back to sleep. See you, Toshi. Hang in there."

What do you mean, hang in there? Am I the only one who has to *hang in there*? Terauchi's coolness bothered me, and I couldn't help but get angry at her. Like she felt she was okay because she'd just been an observer all along. So I pushed down hard on the End button on my phone. This was the last contact I ever had with her, pressing down hard on the button to end the call. The sensation stayed in the pad of my thumb for a while. In contrast, when I called Yuzan next she made me feel encouraged, but at the same time, got me even angrier.

"Kirarin's dead?" Yuzan shouted, and burst out in tears. "How could this happen? I-I won't stand for it. I'm gonna kill that Worm myself!"

"Well, okay, but Yuzan . . ." I said. "I feel responsible for Kirarin's death. I made a huge mistake."

"But *I'm* the one who's most guilty. I took the bike to Worm, gave him the cell phone, so it's *my* fault. Don't blame yourself, Toshi. You have to remember that Kirarin went on her own to meet up with him, so in a sense she brought it on herself. All of us were kind of enjoying his escape. It's a shock that Kirarin died, but don't let it get to you that much. All of us will take responsibility. You don't need to suffer over it alone."

As I listened to Yuzan, I suddenly realized that the shattering of the glass I'd heard next door was the beginning of the end of the world. Ever since that day things had gradually been changing, and today was the final blow. Things couldn't possibly go any lower. I recalled how Terauchi's voice sounded like it was filtering up from underground. But Kirarin's death was too much of a shock for me to dwell on anything. I fell back on my bed. Kirarin—are you really dead? It came back to me—her overlapping teeth showing when she smiled, that lively look she always had when she was startled. I started to cry. She really was dead, after all. I couldn't believe I'd never see her again.

"Toshi, are you okay?"

Yuzan's worried voice called out from the cell phone that I was still clutching. I nodded again and again but couldn't stop the tears. I suddenly noticed that my door was open and that my mother was standing there, looking pale.

"Don't you think you should go to Miss Higashiyama's house?"

"I'll call you back," I told Yuzan, and hung up. She was in tears, too, and couldn't reply.

I called Kirarin's house but all I got was some woman who just kept gloomily repeating that she didn't know anything, that the day for the funeral hadn't been set. I didn't know what to do and paced back and forth in my room.

Reporters started calling us around ten a.m., and I shut my curtain tight. Next, Worm's father stopped by. He said that before he went to see his son in the hospital in Nagano, he wanted to find out from me what had been going on between Worm and Kirarin. He was gaunt, like a sad old man—so much for the former dandy with his ascot. The arrogant face he used to make as he walked past our house was nowhere to be seen.

"What sort of relationship did my son and Miss Higashiyama have?" he asked.

"I really don't know," I lied.

"Is that so," he muttered back, then suddenly fell to his knees on the floor of our dirty entrance.

"I am truly, truly sorry for all the trouble we've caused you. I don't know where to begin to apologize for the death of your friend. Please forgive us. I know my son will spend the rest of his life trying to redeem himself for what he's done to all of you. I should have supervised him more carefully, and since I didn't, this horrible tragedy has taken place, and now I can only hand my son over to the courts. I feel so sorry I don't want to go on living."

This middle-aged man was apologizing to me, a high school girl, for his son. You got it wrong, I wanted to tell him. It was like a game we were playing with Worm. And your wife's murder was part of the game we were enjoying. I stood there, silent, with no idea how I should act. None of this, though, meant very much after I learned that Terauchi had died.

"Why don't you have a bite to eat? You haven't touched anything since this morning." It was almost evening when my mother came up to see me as I lay on my bed, weeping. Just when I started downstairs the phone rang. I motioned to my mother that I'd take it. I had a hunch it was for me. The phone rang on, like it was specifically waiting until I got downstairs.

"Toshiko? I'm afraid I have some terrible news. Kazuko just

killed herself. She left a letter addressed to you. Can you come over right away and open it?"

My brain just went totally blank. I'd heard people say this before, and that's exactly what happened. A total whiteout. I was so shocked it was like I forgot how to move my arms and legs.

The undertaker, with this pained expression, set down the tray used to offer incense. After a quick autopsy, Terauchi's body was back home. And there she was, lying in a coffin. Her face was covered with a white cloth. I just kept staring at her fingers, the blackish fingertips clasped at her chest. When she fell she must have hemorrhaged inside. Maybe they weren't showing her face because it'd been injured. Her beautiful face—what had happened to it now? You dummy, jumping off a building like that! Now we can't see you. How am I supposed to say good-bye if I can't see your face?

"What did she say in her letter?" Terauchi's mother asked me again.

"She said not to show it to anybody else, so I don't think I should," I was finally able to reply. Next to me, my mother stirred, like she was bothered by this. I knew exactly what she wanted to say to me: You know that's not right, Toshiko. This is Terauchi's mother we're talking about. Show it to her. Tell her what she wants to know.

"I understand. It's just that I'm her parent and would like to know what she wrote."

Terauchi's mother's shoulders slumped as she muttered this. I thought maybe it would be okay to tell her the main points of the letter, so I scanned it again, but I'm lousy at summarizing things and nothing of the contents stayed with me. If it were Terauchi doing the summarizing, she'd do a great job, explaining things by emphasizing exactly what mattered. Still, you know something, Terauchi, I wanted to tell her—this is really poorly written. You always were a lousy writer. To really understand this, a person would have to read it a hundred times. Despite all this, I went ahead and tried to explain what was in the letter.

"Mainly what she says is that she's a very philosophical type of person and living exhausted her. There were things that make her and the world incompatible. And she said that as her friend I'm the only one who can understand this, so I shouldn't show it to anybody else."

"Was it studying for entrance exams that did it?" Terauchi's mother asked.

"Maybe. I'm not really sure."

"I understand. This must come as such a shock to you, too, Toshiko. Asking you this must upset you."

Terauchi's mother gave a quick smile. I couldn't imagine what the problems between her and Terauchi had been, but the smile told me that she understood her daughter's feelings.

"Kazuko said this to me," her mother said. "When she heard about Miss Higashiyama's accident she said, 'It's all your fault.' I don't know what she meant by that."

I found that part of Terauchi's letter. *It's too embarrassing to write down.* So you were too embarrassed to even tell me. My mother shook my shoulder.

"Please show her the letter, Toshiko. Kazuko asked you not to, but her parents have the right to see it. It might be addressed to you, but I don't see how you can keep it to yourself."

The right. I wonder about that. It's addressed to me, so doesn't that mean it's just mine? My brain wouldn't function and I just stood there, my mother shaking me. No matter how much she shook me, I still clung tightly to Terauchi's letter. She'd said things about her mother and how turning in Worm and Kirarin to the police made her want to die. The last thing I wanted was for anybody to learn about that. Especially her mother.

"It's okay," Terauchi's father said, interrupting. "No need to force yourself to show it to us. If those were Kazuko's final wishes then we should respect them. Because I think she's still out there, watching us."

At this we all turned to look at the white wood coffin. She's definitely smiling inside there, I thought, her shattered face grinning. I thought of her pleasant features. When I thought that I'd never see that face again, talking to her just this morning seemed like an illusion. Reality started to fade away.

"Terauchi!! You idiot!!"

A voice shouted from behind us. It was Yuzan, shoulders squared, dressed in her usual T-shirt and work pants. The instant she saw the coffin, she collapsed on the floor in tears.

"How could this happen? Tell me! They said Kirarin's dead, too. What am I going to do?"

You got that right, I thought. What am I going to do, too? I'd never been so confused in my life. I noticed that Yuzan, who usually referred to herself by the rough masculine word *ore*, had switched now to the feminine *atashi*. It was weird, but a strangely calm part of me could notice something like that. Next I had to go over to Kirarin's house in Chōfu. I was sure I couldn't see her face either. The two of them had both been crushed. Completely disintegrated, the two of them. Why? I still couldn't comprehend that all these things had happened. Am I to blame for all this? Did it all happen because I didn't report Worm to the police? Thoughts kept swirling round and round in my head. Worm used my cell phone to call the three of us, Yuzan lent him a bike, Kirarin thought it'd be fun, so she went to see him, and Terauchi reported them to the police. This is crazy. Wasn't there an anime movie like this? *Rinbu/Rondo* or something? Kind of out-of-date, I guess. I started to feel faint, but unlike in a movie, I didn't lose consciousness. My head was, in a strange way, totally clear.

Everything about the second semester of my senior year in high school felt cold and distant. I hadn't seen my classmates since the summer break began and they were all too busy to sit down and talk about my two friends that had died. My class was clearly divided into all sorts of cliques. The bookworms were the most numerous, then came the jocks, the Shibuya clubbers, the Barbie Girls, the nerds, and others, and the deaths of these two girls— Kirarin and Terauchi, who belonged to the one group hardest to fathom—didn't seem to really hit home with anybody else. Kirarin's death had been covered in weekly magazines and on TV talk shows, so girls who were into gossipy stuff like that sometimes checked me out like they wanted to ask me about it, but I pretended not to know anything. Compared with the splashy affair of Worm and Kirarin, Terauchi's suicide didn't stand out much, although one of those dry weekly newsmagazines did have an article once about a classmate of Kirarin's having followed her in death by taking her own life.

"Toshi-chan, you're all skin and bones."

Haru, her hair bobbed now, stood blocking my way. Her new boyfriend had apparently told her he didn't like her Yamamba style, so she'd done a total makeover into a Mod. But because of all the makeup she'd worn, her eyebrows and eyelashes had gotten pretty sparse, and this new style didn't suit her.

"Really?" I touched my cheek. "I didn't notice."

"It's no wonder, though. When I heard about Kirarin and Terauchi I was, like, totally shocked. Which is why I thought I'd change my look and cut my hair. My boyfriend had nothing to do with it. I just thought I'd become the kind of shabby person I'd always made fun of."

"The world's changed for you then?" I asked.

"It has. Or at least the kind of guys who try to pick me up." Haru raised her thin eyebrows as she smiled. "Guys who think I'm some weird creature are always trying to pick me up. At cram school it's nuts. But it doesn't matter—none of them are worth the time, anyway. Toshi, you haven't been to cram school at all. Did you apply for the winter session?"

Not sure how to respond, I stared off into space. Cram school. Entrance exams. Before all this happened those were all I could think about, worrying about how the exams were right around the corner. But now it seemed so far away.

"I don't know yet," I replied.

"Yeah, I hear you. You were pretty close to Kirarin and Terauchi, so it must have been a shock. Y'know, I never really liked Kirarin that much, to tell you the truth. She was kind of a Goody Two-shoes. She went out partying all the time, yet when she was with you guys she pretended to be all serious. I know I shouldn't say this now that she's dead, but her death didn't hit me the way Terauchi's did."

People's deaths really do carry different importance for different people. Everybody pretty much had forgotten all about Worm's mother, and for me, Kirarin's death just made me sad. Sure, it hurt when I thought I wouldn't ever see her again, when I remembered all the times she'd been nice to me, when she'd said something funny. Crying for her was like a conditioned reflex. But Terauchi's death was totally different. Her suicide had a powerful effect on me—it hardened everything in my heart, and drained me. Left me dazed and confused. And I still haven't figured out how to deal with it. It's sad, for sure, but I don't feel like I'm totally empty or anything, more like my mind's a blank still trying to figure out what happened. It was like that hollow feeling had turned me dull. People were always giving me these weird looks and unwanted sympathy.

"What's happened to Yuzan?" Haru asked.

After Terauchi's funeral, Yuzan fell off the grid. Once she called from a bar in Shinjuku 2-chōme and said she had a new girlfriend and wouldn't be coming home anytime soon, and I wasn't to worry if I didn't see her for a while. She was apparently going to lean on her new lover and heal that way. It was also clear that Yuzan had decided to come out of the closet. After Terauchi's funeral it became clear how much it had hurt Yuzan to learn that Terauchi's final letter was written just to me.

"Toshi, is it true that Terauchi left a final letter?"

Right after the funeral, Yuzan came over to me. She had on her school uniform skirt, which she wasn't used to wearing. It was tucked up a bit. She looked bewildered. I was sure Yuzan liked Terauchi a lot, and the fact that Terauchi had died without saying a word to her clearly had shaken her. I couldn't lie. You understand why, right? If I did lie, I'd have to make up some other plausible story, and the last thing I needed was another burden to carry around. Keeping Terauchi's secret was enough of a burden, and it made me feel like I was going to collapse.

"It's true," I said.

I stared down at the floor of the funeral parlor, which reflected the bright light of the chandelier overhead. Kirarin's funeral had been a private affair, but Terauchi's was open and held at a brand-new funeral parlor. All of us—her parents' relatives and in-laws, people from school, classmates—stood out in the courtyard, noisy with the shrill cry of cicadas, to see off her casket. I overheard one middle-aged lady complain that with suicides they usually held private, low-key funerals, but to me this kind of funeral fit Ter-auchi perfectly. An unexpected ending. If Terauchi were here she might have said this and laughed.

"What did she write?" Yuzan asked.

I quickly gave her the kind of perfunctory answer I'd given Ter-auchi's mother. Yuzan bit her lip in frustration.

"Really. So she didn't say a thing about me?"

"She didn't write about anybody else. Just about her own per-sonality."

"Then why'd she address it to you? And not her old lady?"

Yuzan looked blank. I shook my head.

"I have no idea. Nobody ever knew what was in Terauchi's head."

"I wonder," Yuzan said, and then was silent.

But I think *I* understood her, Yuzan probably wanted to add. If Kirarin had lived she probably would have said the same thing as Yuzan. Terauchi might have tried to deceive us, but sometimes we liked her warped attitude and offbeat sense of humor. And some-times we almost painfully felt these were our own.

"Ah—this is so, so hard. Man—everybody's gone."

Yuzan wiped her tears away with her palm like guys do. I'm still here, I wanted to say, but couldn't. It was like Yuzan and I were saying good-bye, each of us on opposite shores with Terauchi's letter standing between us.

"I feel so lonely," I said.

"You shouldn't, Toshi. You should be happy 'cause you still have your whole family and everything."

I felt pushed even further away from Yuzan. Was I really happy? I asked myself. This person to whom Terauchi's final letter was entrusted? She'd written that she'd uncovered the darkness that lay within her. Terauchi should have uncovered the real me, too. But instead she said farewell. As I stood there vacantly, Yuzan tapped my shoulder.

"About the cell phone, don't worry about it. It was in my name, so you have nothing to do with it. I doubt the cops'll ask you about it."

It *was* kind of strange. According to Worm's dad, when he talked to us three days after Terauchi's and Kirarin's deaths, miraculously Worm had only external injuries, nothing internal. He could talk and was being interviewed by the police. Still, I'd heard nothing from them yet.

"Well, see ya."

Yuzan duckwalked away, her summer school uniform looking uncomfortable on her. She had her usual backpack slung across her shoulder and I noticed a key holder attached to a zipper as I watched her walk away. The key holder had a *purikura* instant photo the four of us had taken when we were fooling around back in the holidays at the beginning of May.

"Miss Yamanaka, I wonder if I could have a word with you."

In the shadows at the entrance to the funeral home the female detective was waiting for me. A little ways off to the side was her partner, the middle-aged man. The woman had on a wide-brimmed white hat and a scarf around her neck, perhaps to keep from getting sunburned. She's just like Candy, I thought, and came to a halt, awaiting judgment.

"I'm so sorry for all these shocking events that have happened to you, one after another. My apologizes for coming to see you at the funeral. Why don't we go over there where it's a bit cooler?"

The two of them motioned me over to the shade beneath some trees in a small park next to the funeral home. The people who'd attended Terauchi's funeral slipped past us, heads drooping.

"I still can't figure out what led to your neighbor and Miss Higashiyama getting together. Her parents said they have no idea, and the boy's father said the same. Miss Higashiyama's contact list didn't contain your neighbor's number at all."

I summoned up the courage to ask, "The boy next door didn't have a cell phone?"

He didn't, the detective said as she glanced at her notepad. Great. Worm threw it away. I wanted to dance for joy, but soon felt ashamed at caring only about saving my own neck.

"It surprised me, too," I said. "Maybe they just happened to hook up."

"I wonder about that."

The female detective looked up, doubt in her eyes. The old man spoke up.

"The boy said the same thing, but you and Miss Higashiyama were friends, and the only thing I can think is that you helped bring them together."

"I don't know anything about it," I said.

"But you talked on the phone with Miss Higashiyama the day before she died," the female detective said.

All of a sudden it hit me that this was just like something else

I'd experienced before. Those pushy canvassers in front of the station. Guys with their questionnaires, women clutching clipboards. Young girls practicing to be fortune-tellers. *Tell a lie.* Come on, Ninna Hori, you can do it! Acting's your forte. You're the only one who's going to protect yourself. I could hear Terauchi whispering this to me.

"There was just something I needed to ask her. I had no idea where she was. We just talked about movies and stuff like always and then I hung up."

Cold sweat was running down from my underarms. I was trying my hardest to cover up something, but I knew it wasn't just my own guilt.

"Is that right?" the woman said, a disappointed look on her face. "I'm also wondering whether Miss Terauchi's suicide might not also be connected to this affair. We know she talked with Miss Higashiyama, and all I can think is that they argued about her being together with the boy."

"Terauchi wasn't that kind of person," I insisted. "What I mean is, the kind of person who would die for somebody else. She wasn't stupid. She was much smarter than that, very sensitive, the kind where you weren't sure if she was completely unattractive, or the total opposite. But she's not the kind of person who would die over something dumb like that."

As I was speaking I started to cry. The weird thing was, this was the first time I'd cried over Terauchi. The woman looked concerned and frowned.

"I'm very sorry. We'll ask you about this at some other time. Still, it's all very puzzling," she said, catching the eye of her partner. The old guy nodded and brushed away a mosquito.

"We heard that Miss Terauchi left behind a letter. I wonder what was in it. We actually had a call come in with information that led us to the two of them, and I have the feeling it was Miss Terauchi who made the call. I sense that since you were all good friends, when you found out the boy next door had run away you got together to help him. I'm guessing that Miss Terauchi found out about this and got angry, called the police, and when Miss Higashiyama was killed in that unfortunate accident, she felt responsible and took her own life."

I was taken aback. It sounded so stupid when someone else put it into words. Which is exactly why I had to lie. Not to protect myself so much as to protect the truth about how all of us felt when we first heard about Worm. Or to protect what Worm felt in the instant he murdered his mother. Because it was something nobody else could know.

"Don't you think that's taking it a little too far?"

I wiped away my tears, dumbfounded.

"It is a bit much, isn't it?" she said. "I don't think even you all would do something that stupid."

The detective's tone was sarcastic, but it didn't bother me. I'd seen her close her notepad, so I knew she'd given up on pursuing it further.

"Well, we're off to question the boy."

And that was the last time the police ever came by.

I was standing there blankly, thinking of all that had happened at Terauchi's funeral. Haru was waving her hand right in front of my face.

"Hey, you all right? You look really out of it."

"I'm okay. It's just that lots of things have happened."

"When everything's back to normal come back to the cram school, okay?"

Haru said this gently as she pulled up her loose socks, which had slipped down. "Bye-bye," I told her, then realized with a wry smile that those had been Terauchi's last words.

When I got home there was a letter waiting for me on top of my desk, from some guy I didn't know. What is this? I thought. I sat down at my desk, gathered myself together, and opened the envelope. Even now, every time I see a sealed letter it gives me the creeps.

Dear Miss Yamanaka,

I'm sure you're very surprised to get a letter out of the blue from someone you don't know. My name is Wataru Sakatani, and I'm a student at Waseda University. I used to go out with Kirari Higashiyama and I got your address from her mother. I hadn't heard from Kirari for a long time, and it was a real shock to hear about this terrible accident. I can't believe, even now, that she's actually gone. It's so sad.

I learned of her death when the police came to my house. They came because the day before she died, I got a call from the suspect. Also, on the day of her death, I was worried about her and called her cell phone. The first call she made was on the hotel's records, and the call I made the day she died they found on her cell phone records.

I don't know much about what happened but I somehow feel I'm to blame. I haven't been able to say this to anyone else (meaning, I don't think they'd understand—not that I'm trying to hide my mistakes), but I decided to tell you everything.

To go into more detail, I can't help but think that it was my phone calls that got Kirari into that accident. Or that maybe this all happened because our relationship had gone bad.

I called her cell phone simply because I was worried that something had happened to her, and at first she sounded happy, but by the end she seemed sad. I wanted to suggest that we start going out again, but that weird phone call the day before made me worry she'd changed too much, so I didn't say anything. I had doubts about her. For a moment I thought I'd call her again, but I didn't. But if I had called her a second time, if I had asked her to see me again, maybe she wouldn't have gone with that boy.

I don't think this kind of speculation is pointless. I'm sure I'll be thinking about her for the rest of my life. All the what ifs and if onlys . . . Anyone who says I should stop thinking about these kinds of things doesn't have burdens himself. Or else is a person who never had a decisive moment in his life. I've been thinking about all kinds of things, and I've decided I'm going to live with this burden for the rest of my life. I'm sure there will be times when that feeling will be strong, and other times when it isn't.

When I heard from Kirari's mother that her good friend Terauchi had taken her life on the same day, I felt very, very sorry for you, Miss Yamanaka. I imagined that, even more so, you must be suffering, wondering *what if*. If that's the case, then I truly feel sorry for you. As I said before, all we can do is live with our burdens (though maybe you don't have any). To live and *imagine*. That's the job left for those of us who've survived.

Maybe I've said too much. But it helps me a lot to write to you. Thank you for reading what I had to say.

Yours,
Wataru Sakatani

I took out Terauchi's last letter from my drawer and lined it up with Wataru's. There was something, I wasn't sure what, that the two of them shared.

We're in the same boat. What I mean is, you have to deal with my death.

I'm dealing with it already, I said to her. Bye-bye, Terauchi. Those of us who've survived—me, Worm, and Yuzan—will remember you and Kirarin for the rest of our lives. Wataru will remember Kirarin. And the man next door will never forget his wife.

A sudden thought hit me. The next time I go to karaoke, I'm through with using a fake name. No more Ninna Hori. Tears welled up in my eyes, and my name written by Terauchi on the envelope—*Miss Toshiko Yamanaka*—was blurry.

A NOTE ABOUT THE AUTHOR

Natsuo Kirino, born in 1951, is the author of sixteen novels, four short-story collections, and an essay collection. She is the recipient of six of Japan's premier literary awards, including the Mystery Writers of Japan Award for *Out,* the Izumi Kyōka Prize for Literature for *Grotesque,* and the Naoki Prize for *Soft Cheeks.* Her work has been published in nineteen languages worldwide; several of her books have also been turned into movies. *Out* was the first of her novels to appear in English and was nominated for an Edgar Award. She lives in Tokyo.

A NOTE ABOUT THE TRANSLATOR

Philip Gabriel is professor of Japanese literature at the University of Arizona. He has translated works by Kenzaburō Ōe, Senji Kuroi, Akira Yoshimura, Masahiko Shimada, and Haruki Murakami, including Murakami's *Kafka on the Shore; Blind Willow, Sleeping Woman* (cotranslator); *Sputnik Sweetheart;* and *South of the Border, West of the Sun.* Gabriel is a recipient of the PEN/Book-of-the-Month Club Translation Prize (2006), and the Japan-U.S. Friendship Commission Prize for Translation of Japanese Literature (2001).

A NOTE ON THE TYPE

This book was set in Caledonia, a typeface designed by W. A. Dwiggins (1880–1956). It belongs to the family of printing types called "modern face" by printers—a term used to mark the change in style of the type letters that occurred around 1800. Caledonia borders on the general design of Scotch Roman but it is more freely drawn than that letter. This version of Caledonia was adapted by David Berlow in 1979.

COMPOSED BY

Creative Graphics, Inc.,

Harrisburg, Pennsylvania

DESIGNED BY

Iris Weinstein